THE HOUSE OF LONG AGO

Also from Steve Berry

Cotton Malone Novels
The Warsaw Protocol
The Malta Exchange
The Bishop's Pawn
The Lost Order
The 14th Colony
The Patriot Threat
The Lincoln Myth
The King's Deception
The Jefferson Key
The Emperor's Tomb
The Paris Vendetta
The Charlemagne Pursuit
The Venetian Betrayal
The Alexandria Link
The Templar Legacy

Stand-alone Novels
The Columbus Affair
The Third Secret
The Romanov Prophecy
The Amber Room

Steve Berry and M.J. Rose
The House of Long Ago
The Lake of Learning
The Museum of Mysteries

Also from M.J. Rose

Cartier's Hope
Tiffany Blues
The Library of Light and Shadow
The Secret Language of Stones
The Witch of Painted Sorrows
The Collector of Dying Breaths
The Seduction of Victor H.
The Book of Lost Fragrances
The Hypnotist
The Memoirist
The Reincarnationist
Lip Service
In Fidelity
Flesh Tones
Sheet Music
The Halo Effect
The Delilah Complex
The Venus Fix
Lying in Bed

M.J. Rose and Steve Berry
The House of Long Ago
The Lake of Learning
The Museum of Mysteries

THE HOUSE OF LONG AGO

A Cassiopeia Vitt Adventure

By Steve Berry and M.J. Rose

The House of Long Ago
A Cassiopeia Vitt Adventure
By Steve Berry and M.J. Rose

ISBN: 978-1-952457-05-0

Published by Blue Box Press, an imprint of Evil Eye Concepts, Incorporated

Now ye may suppose that this is foolishness in me;
but behold I say unto you,
that by small and simple things are great things brought to pass.

Alma 37:6
Book of Mormon

Chapter 1

GIVORS, FRANCE
FRIDAY, MARCH 8TH
10:00 A.M.

I LOVE ART.

Always have.

That appreciation had been bred into me as a young girl from a father who'd adored everything and anything associated with the creative mind. He'd loved it all. Painting. Sculpture. Writing. Architecture. He'd never discriminated and taught me that every piece of art, no matter how odd or repulsive, carried significance. So I was intrigued that the morning's mail had brought an invitation to an exhibition.

Like a new baby coming into the world.

The name of the show *Le Marché de l'Art sous l'Occupation, The Art Market During the Occupation,* along with its date and location, were superimposed over a vintage black and white photo of a crowded auction from long ago, an auctioneer holding up an elaborately framed painting for the audience to inspect. In white type along the bottom was the legendary name Charpentier and a date.

1944.

I knew Charpentier.

A Paris auction house of long standing.

As a child I'd often accompanied my father on collecting jaunts and auction houses had been one of his many haunts.

I'd visited Charpentier several times.

The opening of the new exhibition was in twelve days' time, on

March 20th at the Shoah Memorial Museum in Paris, and an enclosed note was handwritten in black ink on a cream-colored notecard.

Mademoiselle Cassiopeia Vitt,
it would be our pleasure if you could attend
and have your father with us in spirit.

The exhibition sounded interesting and the personal sentiment touched me.

But only for a moment.

It's sad how cynical I'd become.

Yet experience had taught me that most invitations like this came with an ulterior motive. I'd inherited not only my father's love of art and history but his entire fortune and estate, which included both his multinational corporation, Terra, and his private foundation, which helped fund art programs in elementary schools and provided scholarships at several universities, even offering a finance sponsorship position to select museums. Consequently, I was often invited to join the boards of art institutions around the world.

And attend auctions.

This invitation was probably the first step in an effort to entice me into becoming a donor. Since I wasn't planning on being in Paris any time in March, I laid the invite in a pile for my assistant to deal with, who would RSVP that I was sorry but could not attend.

No other mail needed my attention so I poured a fresh cup of coffee from the silver carafe on my desk and perused my daily newspapers. *International New York Times*, *Herald Tribune*, *Figaro,* and *Le Monde*. I'd long ago abandoned hard copies, preferring now to review them all on line.

Both of the French papers contained extensive reports on a robbery that had sent shock waves through the art world. Sometime last week audacious bandits had tunneled through a hillside and entered Anne and Philip de Parka's villa in Provence through the basement. Undetected, they made off with more than twenty million euros' worth of sculpture including works from Rodin, Henry Moore, Degas, Giacometti, and Brancusi. The Parkas only used the villa as a weekend escape and were not there during the break-in. Nor did they become aware of the robbery until four days after it happened. There had been a highly sophisticated security system, but nothing triggered since the thieves entered from beneath through a 15th century cellar that had no outside entry or egress. The incident piqued my interest not only because I knew the Parkas socially, but I too owned a villa near theirs.

But it was no weekend retreat.

Mine was called *Casa de Hace Mucho Tiempo.*

House of Long Ago.

I'd been six years old when my mother, father, and I moved into it.

A place with a story.

My father, Arturo Pedro Cristóbal Vitt, had been a businessman with an historian's knowledge, an artist's soul, and a religious man's ethics. He regarded antiquities, artwork, and architecture with a deep reverence. No wonder he'd fallen in love with the ancient stone structure perched on an outcropping of Spanish rock known as Tossa de Mar, high above the Mediterranean Sea. When he bought the house, it was not inhabitable. Once it had been a monastery, founded in the 11th century by Benedictines, rebuilt several times during the ensuing centuries. During the Spanish Civil War it became a refuge for those being targeted by anarchists and communists. While the Republicans and the fascists, headed by Generalissimo Francisco Franco, fought each other, priests were rounded up and executed daily. The Benedictine monks, who by then had returned to the site, took in those at risk and hid them. The war lasted almost a year and more than a million died, but hundreds of innocents were saved by the monks of Tossa de Mar.

As a child I became obsessed with the heroics of those robed holy men, many of whom were buried in the cemetery on our lush grounds. We owned forty acres of ruins, forest, olive groves, and a steep rocky staircase that led down to a secluded cove. A fifteen-minute drive led to the 14th century walled city of Tossa de Mar with its seven watchtowers, and a forty-minute ride brought you to Barcelona.

The monks' main claim to fame for over three centuries had been olive oil. Presses, bottles, baskets, and other paraphernalia needed in its manufacture had been found on the grounds during my father's four-year-long renovation. Most of the larger stone items were salvaged, some used as sculptural elements in my mother's garden, others as decorations throughout the grounds. My parents died a long time ago and, for the past couple of years, I had been deliberating on the idea of selling the property. I rarely ventured there much anymore. I lived in France, so the villa had sat idle for a long time. And it wasn't just that I didn't want to let it go that kept me from calling in the realtors, it was that so many memories would be stirred.

Some wonderful, of course.

Most, in fact.

But some were sad, others brutal and frightening.

No one amassed a fortune the size of my father's without making enemies. I recall how more than once someone had tried to destroy him. How they even used my mother and me on occasion in their efforts. But after reading about the robbery in Provence, I knew that even if I wasn't ready to sell the house, it was time to divest it of its most valuable possession—my father's *Galería de Belleza,* his Gallery of Beauty—a collection of fifteen special paintings that he'd treasured, each a masterpiece, each carefully chosen and lovingly conserved.

By both him in life.

And me, after his death.

Chapter 2

FOUR DAYS LATER

THE DAY STARTED OFF WARM IN SOUTHERN FRANCE AND BECAME EVEN warmer when my corporate jet landed in Barcelona. Minutes later I was in the rear seat of a Mercedes on the way to Tossa de Mar.

I rolled down the car windows and allowed the fresh sea air to wash over me.

My driver navigated the familiar roads with ease and I allowed the coast to welcome me home. I'd made arrangements to meet my friend Miguel Velez at my parents' house. He served as the deputy director of conservation and research at the Prado Museum in Madrid. I wanted him to inspect my father's art collection as to condition and value. My plan was to split the paintings between the Prado and the Louvre—the two museums my father had been most involved with—donating them in perpetuity.

I arrived two hours before Miguel, greeted by Angelina Costes, our longtime housekeeper, and her husband, Paulo, who served as groundskeeper. For thirty years they'd lived in a cottage on the property and taken care of the estate. Both were now up in age, nearing retirement, which was another reason why I knew I had to make some changes. I couldn't count on them staying around forever, and it would be next to impossible to find two more trustworthy people.

The last time I'd come, three months ago, it had been for a short visit with someone special. Harold Earl "Cotton" Malone was my boyfriend. Strange that I attached such a descriptive term to a man. But facts were facts. He was the love of my life. Or at least I'd come to believe that.

We'd spent a few days at the villa, adding to my inventory of wonderful memories from the place.

The car stopped and I stepped out into the bright sun.

Angelina was waiting and looked disappointed to see I was alone. I knew she'd been taken with Cotton's Southern charm. Who wouldn't be? He had that way about him. Like Churchill said, *Tact is the ability to tell someone to go to hell in such a way that they look forward to the trip.* He always said his mother had that ability, and he seemed to have inherited the skill too. When he'd accompanied me to the house he'd spent most of his time in my father's library. About the only thing that had drawn him away had been Angelina's *crema catalana,* a traditional custard finished with a caramelized sugar crust. It had been one of my father's favorites too. Cotton loved books and owned a rare bookshop in Copenhagen. My father had also been a lifelong bibliophile. Many of the books he'd bought as a young man became, over time, quite valuable. *In the hundreds of thousands of euros*, Cotton had said after his inspection. Last year I'd donated an original Elizabethan quarto valued at over a quarter of a million euros to the Bodleian Library. I planned to make a lot more donations too.

"No *Señor* Malone?" Angelina asked.

"Not this time."

"That is too bad. But it is good to see you, *señorita.*"

This was going to be tough. I'd come to discuss my father's art collection with Miguel, preparing to divest myself of both it and everything else my parents owned, including the house. My mother died eighteen years ago in a car accident. My father, who'd been ten years older, passed a year later from what many believed was a broken heart. It had taken me a long time to recover from losing them, especially with so much between us left unsaid. Late in life my parents had become devoted to the Church of Jesus Christ of Latter-Day Saints. Me? Not so much. And it wasn't anything against their choice of beliefs, it was just that religion was not vital to me. That indifference, as a young adult, had created a rift between us that was only partially repaired before their deaths. More a truce to the war instead of serious peace talks.

With their deaths I became, barely out of university, the owner of a multibillion euro fortune, in total control of one of the largest corporations in Europe. Thank goodness my father had hired a cadre of competent lawyers and managers. The corporation had flourished. Out of respect I'd left the house intact, unwilling to focus on what to do with it, for to do anything meant dealing with my regrets.

But I'd learned that grief is not nearly as hard to bear as regrets.

So the time had come to deal with reality.

My father's art collection was too valuable to remain in any ordinary house under even the best of circumstances.

And these were hardly that.

Paulo, Angelina, and I enjoyed a lunch of grilled fish and fresh salad. The kitchen windows hung open and the scent of the sea mixed with the perfume of the wisteria in the nearly-spring air. I told them my plans and they were glad I was finally selling. Though it was their home, and they wanted to stay, they also wanted to spend more time with their children and grandchildren in northern Spain. We reminisced about the past, laughed, and cried a little. But in the end, we all knew the time had come for the House of Long Ago to belong to someone else.

Miguel arrived on time at 4:00 p.m. and I greeted him at the door.

We'd attended university together and had remained lifelong friends. He was my age, pushing forty, but looked older because of the touch of gray in his tightly curled hair and flaring mustache. He was, as always, impeccably dressed in a light gray suit, linen shirt, and black loafers. He was married to another curator at the Prado and they had two little boys. I often had dinner with them when I was in Madrid, but it had been at least a year since I'd seen Miguel. Even though I'd congratulated him on the phone, I spent the first few minutes exclaiming over his recent promotion to deputy director of the museum.

"I hope my donation winds up being a feather in your cap," I told him over coffee in the living room.

"I'm really honored that you chose me to be the first to see the collection and that you are giving us the pick of the paintings. I knew it was smart of me to befriend you in that art history class."

He sipped his coffee and I watched as his trained eye traveled over the paintings in the living room.

"These are lovely, Cassiopeia," he finally said. "But I'm afraid they're not museum quality."

I laughed. "Of course not. These are paintings my parents found together at various markets and little auction houses when they were younger. I don't think any one of them cost more than a few hundred euros. What they represent are beautiful memories they cherished."

"As all art should. So where are the others?" he asked, not even trying to hide his excitement.

"Let me show you."

I ushered him out of the living room and down a long corridor. Toward its end, I said, "As you know this house was once a monastery. And this—" I opened a door at the end of the hall, "was the cloister."

We walked into a covered stone gallery surrounding a plush interior garden. Paulo had lovingly maintained it through the years, just as my *mamá* had when she was alive. The day's sun shone warm and bright.

"It's beautiful," he said.

"It was always my favorite spot in the house."

We walked down one of the covered sides, past archways that framed the garden. At the end, we reached a set of double-arched wooden doors strapped with iron.

"When *papá* bought the property he was told this room had once been the monks' chapel. On the other side of these walls is the old graveyard. He was also told that the room was no longer consecrated. So he transformed it into a private gallery."

I unlocked the door.

And watched his face take in what lay before him.

Chapter 3

THE INTERIOR WAS ONE UNBROKEN RECTANGULAR SPACE, AN intriguing combination of modern and ancient architecture. The floors and walls were a pale taupe Montjuïc sandstone found in the local mountains. They'd been first crafted centuries ago, then renovated in the 1950s. A triple height ceiling peaked above us, reconstructed out of wood and plaster and colored a bone white. The Gothic windows on the north and south walls, which had only contained shards when we moved in, were now filled with leaded opaque glass that filled the old sanctuary with a spectral, colored glow.

Like from heaven, my father used to say.

There were no pews—those had been missing for a long time—so the only remaining religious aspect was an unadorned sandstone slab that had once accommodated an altar at the east end. Four comfortable beige leather couches ran down the center, alternating how they faced. No other furniture or adornments filled the room. The idea had been to focus on the fifteen masterpieces hanging from the tall walls, and the lighting had been designed to attract one's complete attention.

Six paintings on the north wall. Six on the south. Three on the east.

Their artists were an astounding list of who's who. For my father, buying a work of art was in itself a work of art. He approached each purchase with great care and long scrutiny. He studied art history, but not as a hobby, more a passion. He was an avid gallery and museumgoer, always searching for something new or visiting an old favorite.

And he'd shared those quests with me.

We'd often made pilgrimages to the Prado.

A trip to a museum is a special thing, he always told me.

I recall his rules.

Arrive early. Never try and see everything. Always take your time. Place what you see within its historical context. Discuss it, if possible, with any expert that might be around. And, above all, have fun.

He particularly practiced that last rule.

Questions were his thing.

What do you think the person in the painting liked to do? How would the weather feel if you were inside that landscape? Who do you think used the room depicted? How was it used? If you could spend the day inside of any painting, which one would it be?

I'd loved imagining.

I remember the first time we toured the Louvre. I was seven. We'd arrived at the glass pyramid early on a Monday morning. He was definitely right about arriving early, but the best time to visit any museum was when it opened on a Monday morning. It's the least trafficked hour on the least trafficked day thanks to the exodus of tourists leaving on Sundays after weekend festivities. That morning we were first in line. Once inside, we didn't stop to glance at anything. Instead, my father led the way to the Denon wing and straight to room 711. For five minutes he and I were alone with the Mona Lisa. We stood as close to the painting as allowed and he held me up so I could be eye level with the famous lady.

Watch how she follows you as we move, he said.

He walked me around the gallery, which was starting to fill with visitors. And I saw how the grand lady's eyes seemed to come with me.

Is there a real person behind the wall? I'd asked, not understanding how this effect was possible.

My father chuckled. *Hardly. But when an artist adds his soul in every brushstroke, magic happens. Of all the talents people possess, the talent to create is the most mystical and impressive. We need to pay homage to that, as much as we do to God. That's why we don't just go to church. We visit museums and galleries and study history. All to honor the sacred in this world.*

That had been his mantra—*to honor the sacred in this world.*

And seeing that beautiful mysterious lady created by Leonardo da Vinci follow me around the room, along with the reverence my father paid it, I started to understand what he meant. On his tombstone I had *He honored the sacred in this world* engraved.

It seemed fitting.

And now as I walked Miguel through the gallery, I thought how well my father had done just that.

"According to the last estimate," I said to Miguel, "this collection is worth at least fifty million euros. As I told you on the phone, no matter how well protected this gallery is and how secretive we've been about having such a valuable collection on the grounds, I can't leave it here anymore. Not only because of my fear for its safety, but because I believe these paintings should be enjoyed by all. I know my father would be happy I'm splitting them between the two museums he loved the most."

"I'm overwhelmed," Miguel said as he forced himself to stop staring at the paintings. "*Muchas gracias*, Cassiopeia. Everyone who knew your father said he was a generous man. He'd be so proud of you."

I was quiet for a few seconds, afraid that if I spoke my voice might crack. Finally, I said, "I hope he would be pleased with my decision. I miss him a lot. But less when I'm here." I gestured to the paintings. "Would you like a tour?"

"Absolutely."

We started to the right of the door at a Picasso. It had been painted during his Rose Period, when he used cheerful colors to explore the world of harlequins, clowns, and circus performs. 1904 to 1906, if I remembered correctly. The last time he painted exclusively in a figurative style. I told Miguel how this one featured both a harlequin and an acrobat. With clear reverence, Miguel approached the canvas and stood in silence.

"It's magnificent," he said.

I agreed.

He moved from the Picasso to the next painting, a Klimt of an apple tree filled with golden fruit.

"I was with him when we bought this one," I said. "In Paris at the Hammerstein Gallery. He did a lot of business there. I was about ten, but I remember the day clearly. The gallery owner had a dog, a little apricot poodle named Maxine, and I played with her while my father bought art."

"I assume you have the bills of sales and paperwork for all of these paintings?"

"I don't, but our family lawyer, Esmerelda Fortuna, has everything."

We moved from the Klimt to a Joan Miró, one of his surrealistic dream paintings from the 1920s. Then Miguel stood before the oldest in the collection, an amazing Georges de La Tour of a young girl reading a book by candlelight, the canvas aglow with illumination.

"We would need to—"

He cocked his head and moved closer to the painting.

After a few moments he backed up and inspected it from a distance.

He repeated those motions several times.

"What is it?" I asked.

He stepped back to the Picasso.

"Give me a moment," he said with a frown that suggested something was wrong.

He made his way back around the gallery, inspecting each painting more carefully, again stepping back, then forward.

He moved from the Klimt, to the Picasso, to another Picasso, a Dalí, the Joan Miró, a Goya, two Juan Gris, the Georges de La Tour, a Monet, the Chagall, a Georges Seurat, a Georges Braque a Piet Mondrian and finally, the Paul Signac.

The collection was a curious cross section from vastly different periods. True, the artists were all European, but my father had no particular style favorite. Nor a time frame, except that nothing in the collection had been painted after 1930.

All that mattered was that the work spoke to him.

Otherwise, it is meaningless.

"What is it?" I asked again.

Miguel turned to me. His face was pale and he was biting his bottom lip. "I'm not sure how to tell you this, but not one of these paintings is authentic."

He paused.

"Every one of them is a fake."

Chapter 4

HIS ACCUSATION RANG IN MY EARS.

I looked around at the marvelous collection of masterpieces my father had lovingly amassed.

"That's impossible," I said. "My father had an incredible eye. He only bought from the finest and most reputable dealers, demanding unimpeachable provenance."

"I have no doubt that your father was an honorable man. But, Cassiopeia, these paintings are copies. Amazing copies. But copies nonetheless."

I stared at the Georges de La Tour. My favorite. I'd actually been contemplating keeping it. A similar painting hung in the Frick museum. I'd always loved the countenance of the young girl reading, astonished by the candlelight that illuminated her face, making her hand almost translucent. Incredible what the human eye and hand could do with pigments.

"I grew up with these paintings. I was here when each one came into our home. I watched my father personally hang them."

His face stayed set. "They are not originals. There is no doubt."

"How can you tell without scientifically examining them?"

I knew that many methods existed to determine authenticity. Experts could date microscopic flakes of paint thanks to chemical composition. They could perform a comparative analysis to see if the style conformed to the artist. None of these artists were the least bit obscure so all the relevant information would be in a database. The same analysis could be done with the canvas, dating it, comparing it to other canvases of the same period, even sometimes extracting dust particles from within the fabric's weave. They could also perform the same detective work on the wooden stretchers, nails, and joists.

But Miguel had not done any of those things.

"You are saying all this from just *looking* at them. You're that good?"

With perfume a "nose" was someone with the talent to be able to identify thousands of different scents simply from a sniff. In art there was the "eye." Someone who could see all of the subtleties and nuances.

"I have been wrong before, of course." He pointed at the painting. "But these were not done to fool an expert. Copyists sometimes bake paintings to give them the same craquelure as originals from the era. That's not present here. These were not created to cheat someone. It took me a while to pick up on it, but when you look at the canvas surface, it is just not right. I'm betting that once we take them off the wall, we'll see not all of the stretchers are made of wood that matches in age to that painting's period."

The smallest painting was the Braque, so I had no trouble lifting it off the wall and turning it around. I wasn't the expert that Miguel was, but I am an architectural historian. I know the passage of time degraded materials even in the best and most pristine of circumstances. And Miguel was right. The stretchers were different.

I looked from the canvas to my old friend.

"Paints can be found from almost any time period," he said, "or altered to match that period. It is quite easy to do. With no attempt to deceive being made here, it suggests these paintings were not supposed to fool any expert for resale. Rather, they were duplicated for the pleasure of the owner. This is, in fact, done quite often. Masterpieces are so expensive to insure that many collectors have copies made for display, then stash the real paintings in a vault for safekeeping, or donate them to a museum."

"My father would have never been happy with a copy."

He gestured to the gallery. "Have you enjoyed these paintings?"

"Of course."

"Have they given you pleasure?"

"Absolutely."

"And you never knew they were copies?"

I shook my head.

"So these copies have served their purpose," he said.

I replaced the painting on the wall, then walked away from the Braque and stood in front of the Monet.

Miguel joined me. "Feel free to have another expert examine them and confirm my opinion. I have a few names I can give you."

I waved him off. "That's not necessary. I trust you, Miguel. I saw what you meant about the wood with my own eyes. But I'm baffled as to why my father didn't tell me about the copies."

"Could it have happened when you were estranged?"

It had lasted three years. Perhaps the most painful time in my life, with no relationship with my parents. We eventually reconciled, if not completely, enough that we could move forward.

But death had interrupted success.

"That was a long time ago," I said. "I would like to think *papá* would have eventually told me—if he sold or hid away his collection. And why do either? He never had any financial issues. He was a billionaire, several times over, with no debt. And he wasn't paranoid about theft."

"Let's assume, for the moment, he didn't sell them. Many collectors fear they are targets. Your father might simply have stored the originals away for safekeeping. It's not unusual and sounds like the most logical explanation."

My natural cynicism arose. "And what is the least likely explanation?"

"That they were never originals. That your father bought fakes from the beginning and—"

"That's not possible. He was too savvy. My father was not only a collector and art lover, he was a highly educated man. He could not have been duped into buying so many fakes."

Miguel bowed his head in an old-fashioned way. "I apologize. I know this has to be terribly upsetting news."

"The understatement of the century," I said.

"There is one other possibility," Miguel said.

I'd already considered it. "That the originals were stolen, after my father's death. It has been a long time. Plenty of opportunity."

But I had to remind myself that the villa had a state-of-the-art surveillance system and two people who'd cared for it for over thirty years.

"Paulo and Angelina are beyond reproach."

"Forgive me, Cassiopeia, but trust is a peculiar thing. We believe we know people. But, as with these paintings, sometimes we don't see what is right in front of us."

Chapter 5

WHAT I THOUGHT WAS GOING TO BE A SHORT TRIP TO SPAIN, TO BEGIN the process of settling with the past, had turned into a nightmare. The first thing I did after Miguel left was to call my friend Nicodème, who owned a small museum and who I trusted more than anyone when it came to antiquities. In his eighties, he came from a long line of curators and art experts. He'd been one of my father's closest friends and remained that with me.

"Few of those scenarios make sense, Cassiopeia," Nicodème said after I'd explained through the phone all of the possibilities Miguel had offered as to why the paintings weren't authentic. "But first, and foremost, your father would have never bought fakes."

I pictured him in his crowded shop, located in the mountain town of Èze in southern France, surrounded by odd and unique treasures, staring into his "thinking glass," the crystal obelisk that he kept on his desk.

"Miguel does have an incredible eye," he said. "Your father did as well. I think the first thing you need to do is call in another expert and have the paintings examined and tested. I know you said many of the stretchers look new, but that's certainly not conclusive. If an original is damaged, an old canvas can be re-stretched on new wood without it affecting the value of the painting at all. So get them checked. I can suggest a name."

I could tell he was smiling. I can be impatient. He knew that about me, as did Cotton, who always warned me to slow down and study things before I made a move. Advice which, though I knew was right, I often found difficult to follow.

After we hung up, I put in a call to the expert Nicodème had suggested. She was in London, so I offered to send our corporate jet for her if she could rearrange her schedule and meet with me the following day.

Dr. Wanda Smith seemed a diminutive woman.

She arrived at the villa from England carrying a large aluminum suitcase which opened to reveal a traveling chemist's shop, complete with a sophisticated microscope she set up in the gallery. One by one, she scanned a black light across each painting. Then, with a small knife and tweezers, she removed tiny paint samples from the bottom edge of each, which she studied under the microscope.

"Every one of the stretchers appears to be no more than thirty or forty years old," she said. "But their authenticity is not an issue. Many reasons exist for replacements. Insect damage could seriously threaten the painting. Extreme moisture or heat could warp a stretcher. It's even possible the entire gallery had, at some point, endured a weather or water incident and your father had been required to re-stretch all of the paintings."

I was glad I'd listened to Nicodème. As much as I trusted Miguel and knew he had a great eye, something was preventing me from accepting his conclusion that all of the masterpieces were fake.

Three hours later she finished her assessment.

"None of the paintings are originals," she said. "I'm so sorry, *Mademoiselle* Vitt. Every aspect of the inspection shows the same thing. Casting aside the issue of the wood stretchers, it is indisputable that the paint used to create every one of these is less than fifty years old. I also found that each canvas has the same weave and weight and is no more than fifty years old either. I examined dust caught in some of the threads and didn't see what I would if the paintings were authentic."

Like a medical patient getting terrible news and not ready to accept it, I tried to come up with a plausible reason as to why the woman was wrong. "Is it possible that the various sections you studied had been restored? Or the dust and debris you were looking for had been removed in cleaning?"

She shook her head. "That's why I examined them with black light first—to make sure I didn't take samples from restored areas. In fact, that's another red flag. There are no restored areas on any of the paintings. That's not that unusual on the early 20th century works, but it's almost inconceivable with 17th century works. I know what kind of shock you must be in. I'm sorry. It is devastating to discover a crime, or deception, like this in your own home."

"What do you mean deception?"

"There are many instances where paintings are copied and switched during the owner's lifetime for a variety of reasons. Usually financial. And the heirs aren't aware of it."

"My father wouldn't have needed to sell any of these paintings for financial reasons."

Dr. Smith nodded sympathetically, but I could sense that she had seen situations like this before, probably viewing my protestations as emotional reactions to the shock of what had now been confirmed. "All I can say is that it happens more often than you think."

I thanked her for her time and promised a check would be forwarded to cover her fees and expenses.

After she left, I sat alone in the gallery.

I suddenly missed my parents in a way I had not in a long time. I desperately wanted to talk to my father. To have him explain. Because the one thing I was certain of was that he'd not been duped into buying fakes. So what had happened? Had the originals been stolen? In my father's lifetime? Or since he died? Were Angelina and Paulo somehow involved?

That seemed unthinkable.

The Costes were family.

Alone in my room I found my phone and called Cotton. He was in Poland doing god knows what. Three rings and his phone went to voicemail. I left a message, first telling him I was fine. That was a habit we'd both gotten into when apart. All too often one of us wound up in a dangerous situation so we always started a call by reassuring the other we were okay. I was about to tell him that I had some disturbing news, then changed my mind. I didn't want to leave that kind of information in a message. I also didn't want him concerned about me while he was working. He didn't need the distraction.

Instead, I wanted him to stay safe.

So I reassured him all was well, said I just wanted to say hi, and hung up.

I sat on the edge of my bed in the room where I'd spent the first half of my life. Most of the décor from my childhood remained. The four-poster bed, nightstands and dresser, all fashioned in a warm pomegranate shade that still possessed, after so many years, great depth and clarity. Each piece had been made here by local craftsmen. My appreciation for things of old had definitely started in this room. Most appealing had been the drawers, lined with cedar, and I could still smell in my mind that sharp aroma, though in actuality the scent had faded long ago. I'd particularly loved all of the secret compartments that had been added. As a child, they'd fueled my imagination of things lost.

I loved this room.

I'd never had the will or desire to change it in any way.

Which reminded me that I was a big girl now.

Who knew how to handle herself.

So I made another call.

Chapter 6

IT WAS ONLY A FEW KILOMETERS FROM OUR VILLA TO THE TOWN OF Tossa de Mar.

I was glad for the drive along the coast. It calmed me down. I knew dinner would help too. Talking to Jocasta Fortuna always did. We'd attended primary and secondary school together. She and her mother, my godmother, who as a child I called Aunt Esmerelda although we were not related, were prominent lawyers who often worked cases together. For the past thirty years her mother had represented both my father, then his estate.

I parked my car and walked to Bar La Lluna, a cozy little place tucked into an ancient stone building on a charming street in the older part of town. The tapas bar was a perennial favorite, extra crowded when I walked in. I was surprised to see Jocasta already seated at a table in the corner. Never was she early. Rarely on time.

Except today.

We embraced with big hugs and cheek kisses.

She'd already ordered a pitcher of sangria and poured me a glass as I sat. Outside of Spain the drink was usually made with inferior wine and plenty of sweet juices. Junk. Made the authentic way, as in Spain, it was ambrosia. Jocasta lifted her glass and offered a toast to old friends.

I savored a sip. Tart. Tangy.

Perfect.

We started talking as old friends do, without preamble, as if we'd seen each other just yesterday, not over four months ago. She had a delightful new story about her six-year-old twin girls, followed with serious complaints about her ex-husband. The waiter sauntered over and we gave him our order.

She then finished her tale of woe.

"You're being unusually quiet," she said at the end. "Is everything all right?"

And so I told her.

Over plates of tomatoes and mozzarella, mixed olives, fried baby squid, meatballs and chorizo, we talked through all of the possible scenarios as to why paintings that I had believed all my life to be genuine were in fact fakes. Another pitcher of sangria and a half-dozen plates of tapas later, Jocasta suggested I come to the law office in the morning and talk with her mother.

"I'm happy to, but why? I don't think this has anything to do with her."

"Maybe not. But she might know something you don't. She knew your father well, and she is the estate's lawyer. She also drew the will."

"That was all so straightforward," I said. "All of my parents' worldly goods, real estate, business enterprises, everything, was left to me. My mother was an only child and my father set his sister up with a trust many years before."

She smiled. "I know all that. I have been around since you and I were six years old."

She was right. Still—

"My parents did not keep secrets from me. And other than their religious fervor, we saw things similarly. I'm finding this all much more upsetting than I thought I would. The paintings are part of my past with *papá*—"

I stopped speaking.

The wine had relaxed me to the point that I wasn't as in control of my thoughts as I preferred.

Jocasta took my hand in hers.

"Come tomorrow. You never know. Maybe my mother will remember something that could help. Anything would be good, wouldn't it?"

I returned to the villa at ten and was asleep by eleven, but was awoken by my phone at midnight.

I'd forgotten to shut off the ringer.

"Did I wake you?" Cotton asked after my groggy hello. "I can call back in the morning."

"No, it's okay," I said, sitting up in bed. "I want to talk to you. I miss you."

"Me too," he said. "I heard the tone of your voice on the message you left. Something's wrong. What is it?"

He could read me in a way no one else could. Which was just another reason why I loved him. So I told him what had happened and took him through all of the possible explanations I'd come up with to explain the fakes.

"It could definitely have been an inside job that occurred since your parents' deaths," he said. "I like Angelina and her husband a whole lot, and I know you trust them, but what about their kids?"

"It's not possible. Their daughter is a history teacher and their son is a chef in Madrid. We grew up together."

"Maybe you should check them out."

"Are you serious?"

"One of them might have taken advantage of the situation. It wouldn't be that complicated, would it? They could have come to visit their parents and taken photos of the paintings. Then hired a copyist. They would not be hard to find. Once the duplicates were ready, one of them took their parents out to dinner, the other pulled up in a truck. Your villa is so isolated no one would see the exchange of real for fake. The whole job could be done before anyone finished the dessert course. Once home, everything would look fine to Paulo and Angelina."

I shivered.

He made sense. Like always.

"What you say is possible, but not likely."

I couldn't help thinking how devastated Angelina and Paulo would be if it turned out their children had masterminded a robbery.

"Have you told Angelina and Paulo anything about the paintings yet?" he asked.

"There's been no reason to."

"Good. Don't. You need to investigate those kids without alerting them. Esmerelda can help you find someone local."

"I'm seeing her tomorrow. So I can ask. But I don't like this line of thinking."

"I wouldn't imagine you do. It's never comfortable to find out that people who we think we know turn out to be strangers."

No, it wasn't.

Chapter 7

I WALKED INTO ESMERELDA FORTUNA'S LAW OFFICE TO A WELCOME embrace, inhaling her wonderful Rouge perfume, the same scent she'd been using ever since I could remember.

"You look wonderful," I told her.

And she did.

She was a stunning woman in her late sixties, who carried a youthful glow she claimed was due to her early morning ritual of swimming in the Mediterranean. She was wearing a simple sheath dress in her signature color, a deep blue-red, that lovingly highlighted her charcoal hair—now streaked with gray—and her almost black eyes. Her lipstick carried the same maroon tint and, like her perfume, never changed.

"I should have called as soon as I came to town."

My godmother was the woman I was closest to, bar none, since my own mother had died.

She gestured to the couch by the windows. "All is forgiven. You're here now."

I felt comfortable in this office. During my childhood, when my parents traveled, I'd stay with the Fortunas. Jocasta and I would play under the desk, using law books for building blocks, the letter openers and rulers to stave off soldiers, protecting our castles. When we grew older we'd come here at the end of the day to do our homework, sitting at Esmerelda's round conference table while she finished up work. Between our freshman and sophomore years in secondary school we both interned at the firm for the summer. Working in a law office taught me a lot—mostly that I didn't want to be a lawyer.

Which was good.

Everyone had to find their own way.

And I found mine.

A knock on the door and Esmerelda's assistant entered with a tray that held two china cups of café *con leche* and a plate of English biscuits. I knew that Esmerelda enjoyed that exact combination every day at 11 and 4, and whoever might be with her at the time joined her. When I was little the coffee was mostly milk but, as soon as I turned twelve, I downed the same mixture of high-octane expresso.

"I have been waiting a long time for you and me to have this conversation," she finally said.

I'd told Esmerelda on the phone earlier about the problem. "You've been waiting since my parents died for me to come and ask about the paintings?"

She nodded.

"You knew they were fakes?"

"I did."

"Did Jocasta know?"

She shook her head. "That would be violating a client's confidence."

"She's a lawyer too."

"Just not the lawyer for your parents' estate."

Relief flooded through me. That meant I did not have to investigate Angelina, Paulo, or their children.

Thank goodness.

"Your father told me about the paintings a long time ago and asked me not to tell you until you inquired about them."

I was shocked. "Why would he do that?"

"He did not want to burden you until you were ready."

"I don't understand."

She shook her head. "I'm afraid I don't quite understand either. I questioned him but"—she shrugged before continuing—"for all your father's warmth and caring, he could be quite enigmatic. I learned a long time ago that when he didn't want to explain himself, nothing in the world could get him to open up."

I knew that even better than she did.

My father had been loving, generous, and brilliant. But also stubborn and a bit superstitious. He never did a thing he did not want to do.

"A few years before he died, Arturo told me that the insurance for keeping paintings in the house would be better spent buying more paintings. So he canceled the coverage."

I was horrified that I hadn't known. "So what is that amount I see on the accounting report every year to an insurance company?"

"That's for the house and contents. The library, antique furniture, and your father's other collections. But no artwork. The premium is high, I know, but it would be impossibly higher if even one of those paintings had been included."

I felt foolish. I should have paid more attention and thought it through, but I hadn't. Esmerelda served as the estate's lawyer and, on my request, her firm had always maintained the villa. I received a full accounting at the end of each year. I trusted Esmerelda with my life, so I'd never paid all that much attention to what the auditors said. Since my parents' passing I'd been busy running Terra, living in Givors, and building an authentic French castle, using only materials and techniques from the 13th century. It was a labor of love that seemed to consume my every moment. My childhood home had always stayed at the back of my mind, only occasionally invading to the forefront. And I'd come to realize that I'd intentionally avoided the villa because of its memories.

"Your father felt the paintings had simply become too valuable," Esmerelda said. "So he decided to have them copied and live with what he told me were slightly less wonderful versions, but wonderful nonetheless. He then stored the originals in a safe place."

She stood and walked over to her desk, lifting off a manila envelope. "All the details are in here. I was told to give this to you if you ever came and asked."

"And if I'd never come?"

"I prepared a letter to be given to you in the event of my death."

"Did my mother know?"

She shook her head. "He explicitly instructed me not to tell her unless she discovered the situation. This was to be only for you."

I opened the envelope hoping for a letter, a note, anything from my father. But all I found was a key.

And not just any key.

A ward key.

Like a skeleton key, but with what looked like an oversized E attached to its end. Locks were my thing. I studied them in detail, and the older the better. A warded lock used a set of obstructions to prevent it from opening unless the correct key, with the right notches corresponding to the obstructions, was used. During the Middle Ages ward locks were common. I still saw them at ancient monuments and old churches, and I planned on including them in my castle reconstruction. The problem with ward locks was that any well-designed skeleton key could be made to bypass the obstructions. They did not present much of an obstacle to a determined thief. Even worse, there were only a limited number of designs that could be created, so many ward keys were able to open locks they were not designed for.

That's why they eventually became obsolete.

Attached to this one was a string at the end of which hung a white cardboard tag with the letters 368 written on it in black ink.

"What does it open?"

"*El Repositorio.*"

The Repository? "What is that?"

"Cassiopeia, what made you decide to deal with all of this now?"

Not an answer to my question. "I finally realized that the villa has to be sold. I've put that decision off for a long time." I returned to the point. "I'll ask again. What is the repository?"

"Better to show you. Can you arrange for the corporate jet tomorrow morning? Eight a.m.?"

I nodded. "Where are we going?"

"Andorra."

Chapter 8

A CAR AND DRIVER WAITED FOR US AT LA SEU D'URGELL AIRPORT AFTER the short flight from Barcelona. The airport was owned by the government of Catalonia, and though it sat within the municipality of Montferrer i Castellbò, its runways also served the Principality of Andorra, which lay a mere twelve kilometers away. Not a large facility, but adequate enough to accommodate several European carriers, along with a contingent of private planes.

Esmerelda approached the driver and placed her hand on a pad screen. A moment later a ding came and the driver nodded, opening the car's rear doors. Esmerelda and I settled into the seat with a couple of bottles of water. The driver said the trip would take about a half hour.

Andorra was a sovereign, landlocked microstate wedged into the Pyrenees mountains between France and Spain. A place of snow-capped peaks, cascading rivers, cobalt lakes, and lush valleys. Legend proclaimed that Charlemagne created the kingdom for his son, Louis the Pious. A count ruled until the 10th century when the Catholic Church assumed its governance. The present principality came from a 13th century charter that provided for two ruling princes. One, the Catholic bishop of Urgell in Catalonia. The other the president of the French Republic. And though now the government was an elected parliamentary democracy, oddly the co-princes remained.

I'd always thought it a place of superlatives.

Sixth smallest nation in Europe. Less than five hundred square kilometers. Population only 84,000. Sixteenth smallest country in the world. Its capital, Andorra la Vella, the highest in Europe at over a thousand meters above sea level. Ten million people visited annually.

What I really liked was it had the highest life expectancy in the world.

Eighty-two years old.

Impressive.

Somehow it managed to stay neutral in both the Spanish Civil War and World War II, eventually becoming a tax haven for shoppers and savers. And though not a member of the European Union, the euro ruled supreme.

As did banking secrecy.

We continued driving across the beautiful wooded landscape. A plexiglass panel separated us from the driver, providing a measure of privacy.

"What was the handprint for?" I asked.

"This car has been provided by the Repository," Esmerelda said. "Its location is protected, and only an official car, belonging to the facility, can bring someone there. No one is allowed to visit on their own. After your father died, I was substituted as a member, representing the estate."

"Why wasn't I given that designation, as the sole heir?"

I tried to conceal my irritation.

"Because your father expressly told me not to do that, until you came asking about the paintings."

"Any idea why he imposed that condition?"

She shook her head. "Again, he offered no explanation."

We rode for a few moments in silence.

"It's time," the driver's voice informed through a speaker.

Then, Esmerelda said, "We are entering Andorra."

All of the windows clouded, fogged over with something from within, including the plexiglass separator. I had seen this before in glass doors in homes and restrooms that became opaque for privacy, but never in a vehicle.

"It provides a measure of protection for the location, since you are not a member."

"But I'm my father's sole heir," I said again.

"Quite right. Which is the only reason you have been allowed to come."

I found my phone. "I could locate my position with this."

Esmerelda smiled. "You'll find it doesn't work. There is a jamming signal inside this vehicle, which remains in place at the Repository."

We kept riding at a steady speed, still apparently on the main highway.

"Now I can tell you some more information," she said.

I listened as she explained that the Repository was of long standing, dating back to the mid-20th century. A place where the wealthy stored precious metals, art, jewelry, cash, anything and everything of value. Political unrest, wobbly stock markets, unwanted litigation, recessions—all of them created uncertainty. The Repository provided protection against those occurrences as a place of secrecy and safety. One that Andorran law had long sanctioned.

"Why did my father feel the need for it?" I asked.

"I have no idea. He did not share his reasoning with me. I only know that he did utilize the service."

We rode for another twenty minutes, our driver executing a series of turns and at least one roundabout. The fog within the windows dissolved and I saw we were motoring through a dense forest, no houses or towns in sight.

Five minutes later we arrived at a cast iron gate.

The driver rolled down his window and pressed a series of buttons on an electronic keypad. He then stared hard into a lighted sensor for retinal recognition. A few moments later, the gates opened. We drove through, following a narrow, curving road for about two kilometers. Rows upon rows of tall pines and fir trees cast long shadows from the day's bright sun.

"The heavy canopy prevents drone surveillance and further hides the facility," Esmerelda said. "Andorra's mountainous geography is also an element of protection. This is not an easy place to either get to or escape from."

We headed straight for a nondescript stone building. On it were the words *La Vasari Biblioteca.*

"The Repository is inside a library?" I asked.

"Not exactly."

"Vasari was the foremost biographer of artists in the Renaissance," I said, as the driver slowed down. "Is that a coincidence?"

"Hardly. Symbolism is no stranger here."

The car stopped and we stepped out into thin, cool air. The driver stayed behind the wheel, his concentration ahead, eyes focused through the windshield. Esmerelda tapped his window and the man nodded before driving off.

"Does he do tricks too?" I asked.

"They are not hired to be friendly or cordial. They are here as part of the security for the facility."

We climbed three short stone steps.

I have a degree in history and medieval architecture, so I knew this building was 17th century Baroque. Lots of twisted columns, domes, and towers. More curves. Less straight lines. Plenty of oval windows. A beautiful example of the period. Inside, the décor suggested a 19th century renovation, but the Baroque movement from the opulence of the ornaments, stucco, and marble remained. The parquet floors gleamed like a mirror. Persian rugs showed only faint signs of wear. Warm light emanated from amber glass sconces which seemed as welcoming as the faint scent of wax, dust, and old paper that hung in the air.

A young man neatly dressed in a blue blazer, white shirt, and gray slacks waited for us. I looked past him and glimpsed a spectacular reading room with long wooden tables, leather chairs, and antique glass lamps. High above I spotted cameras attached to the beamed ceiling which moved as we did. From a doorway off to the right a woman appeared, about fifty years old, wearing a stylish black Chanel suit, expensive pearls, and nude Ferragamo pumps. Definitely not off the rack attire. She introduced herself as Therese Melia, the Repository's curator.

"Shall we," *Señora* Melia suggested, and she led us through the reading room.

It reminded me of the Bodleian Library at Oxford, where other leather-bound volumes were reverently shelved in a rarified atmosphere.

Cotton would love this place.

We kept going out another doorway and followed a series of twisting corridors that led to an oversized bronze door. *Señora* Melia stepped close to an illuminated pad and stared into the light. A camera mounted high up on the stone wall swiveled on its own and angled downward. Apparently in addition to retinal scanning a visual verification was likewise required to a security office. A red light on the pad shifted to yellow and *Señora* Melia punched in a numeric code.

Triple verification.

The light turned green.

I heard the whir of an elevator. Seconds later the bronze doors opened and the curator gestured for us to proceed inside. The aluminum and steel elevator car had no buttons. Instead, the doors closed and the elevator descended on its own. I was surprised at how long we dropped into the earth.

Finally, we slowed and ended with a gentle thud.

The doors opened and we stepped out into a brightly lit cavernous space. The floor was tiled in gleaming gray squares, the same tone and hue as the rock walls and ceiling. Steel girders were cut into the walls at regular intervals, between which were more steel doors, each with their own illuminated pad like the one above.

"This is the Repository," *Señora* Melia said. "As the sole heir of your father's estate, and pursuant to his express wishes, you are legally entitled to access."

The older woman led us down the lit corridor.

A breeze of fresh, cool air washed over me.

After a short walk we stopped in front of one of the steel doors. A circle, a few centimeters wide, was etched into its surface. At its center was 368. Esmerelda placed her hand onto the adjacent pad and a series of lights above the door blinked yellow, blue, then stopped.

Señora Melia turned to me. "If you would be so kind as to now press your hand on the pad?"

"But I've never been here. You can't have my fingerprints."

"Your father supplied those a long time ago."

A moment from the past flashed across my mind. I was seventeen years old, sitting in *papá's* library with him and some sort of security expert who'd come to the villa to obtain my fingerprints. I asked why they were needed and my father explained that Terra dealt in precious metals, with storerooms containing millions of euros' worth of raw materials. All of them were accessed from fingerprints. As his sole heir, mine were needed to be on file. I never questioned the move. Just accepted it, as a daughter should. Now here I was accessing a vault owned by my father.

Not Terra's. His alone.

I placed my hand on the pad. The lights paced through their dance of color, then the door released.

Señora Melia opened it all the way.

Before us was a small hallway that led to a second steel door. Its frame was sealed in three places with what appeared to be red wax.

"When an owner leaves, after entering their vault, we seal the door with wax. It contains the owner's personal mark."

I stepped close and saw that the red wax held the words Principat d'Andorra and the unique impression of the letters *C T R*.

Choose the Right.

Latter-day Saints sometimes wore a ring with the Choose the Right shield to remind them to be righteous. My father owned such a ring with the same three letters on it, but never wore it. I asked him once about the ring and he said that, to him, the Latter-day Saints themselves were the best examples of their religion. He had no need for symbols. Yet here it was. Part of a seal embedded on a vault door in red wax.

"The owner also dates that seal," *Señora* Melia said.

I saw the date.

From twenty years ago.

"When the owner arrives again, they break the seal themselves. A bit old fashioned, for sure, but we've found it reassuring to our clients." *Señora* Melia gestured us into the sally port. "This is where I leave you. I don't enter the vaults. Do you have your key?"

I nodded and reached into my pocket for the ward key that had come to me from the envelope.

"When you are ready to exit, just close and lock this inner door behind you. I'll be waiting outside."

We thanked her and she left, the outer door shutting, but not locking, behind her. Esmerelda and I were alone.

"Ready?" she asked me.

I slid the key into the door lock and turned.

A metallic click signaled a release.

I opened the door, breaking the wax seals, which crumbled to the floor. Beyond was a room, about four meters square. In the center stood a small table with a black laminate top and two chairs on either side. Against one wall was a familiar sight, the same kind of vertical wooden shelving used in art galleries and artists' studios to store paintings. I recognized the edges of the ornate wooden frames, identical to the ones in our villa.

Relief flooded through me.

Our paintings were here, stored safe and sound.

I approached the first bay of slats. "How long did my father keep the paintings here?"

"From what he told me, as soon as he purchased an original he had it copied. He never kept an original in the villa. They were too valuable and too much a temptation to thieves. He also did not want your home to be a fortress, and all for a few paintings."

I nodded. That sounded like him. Our home had always been filled with wonderful things, but it had also been comfortable to live in every day. I never once felt it a museum. My room had always been furnished exactly as I wanted it, reflecting my interests, tastes, and likes with no questions asked.

I searched the edges of the familiar frames, looking for the one that held my favorite, the Georges de La Tour. I spotted it in the second bay and gingerly slid the compartment forward and stared down at the masterpiece.

But nothing was there.

Only an empty frame.

I reached for another frame, the one that should have held the Rose Period Picasso.

Empty too.

I then examined every one of them.

The paintings were gone.

Chapter 9

I SAT AT THE TABLE WITHIN THE VAULT.

Esmerelda exited through the sally port and I could hear her ask *Señora* Melia to come in. The director protested, but Esmerelda insisted.

"Please examine the frames," I said.

The curator hesitated, then walked over and did just that.

"They are not supposed to be empty," I made clear.

"Are you saying there has been a theft? There is only the one key and you have it. And the seals were unbroken."

"It's a ward key," I said. "They are easily breached."

"But everything else around it is state of the art. The key is simply the final step. A personal touch to the owner. You saw the procedure. It is exhaustive. No one would get this far and be able to use a false key unless we had cleared them. And you saw the seals. They were unbroken, with your father's mark pressed on them."

"Nonetheless, this vault is empty."

The curator was indignant. "We have never had an incident."

"Until now," Esmerelda said. "This was a collection worth tens of millions of euros, and every painting is gone."

"Then *Señor* Vitt must have removed them, because no one has been in this room, other than him, since he first became a client thirty years ago. Our records are clear on that."

I didn't believe a word she'd said. So much time had passed that anyone could have gained access, especially the people who actually operated this repository. An easy matter to use another ward key to open the lock, then replace the wax seals, imprinting the same *CTR* in the wax.

Especially considering my father was dead.

"Who owns this place?" I asked.

"That is confidential."

"It won't be when I take you to court. Or have you charged with theft."

I could see that my words had an effect.

"*Señorita* Vitt, our records indicate that, until today, no one has entered this vault other than your father. Neither I, nor anyone else, has breached the seals. No one."

"We're going to need to see those records," Esmerelda said.

"The logs are available for inspection, per our agreement with clients. But you are not going to find any anomalies."

Probably because whoever managed to accomplish the theft was well versed, with access to those records, able to manipulate them at will. That was the problem with secrecy. It cut both ways. Not only assuring privacy, but creating the perfect environment for corruption.

The curator escorted us out of the vault and to a subterranean office cut from the rock. There was a desk, file cabinets, computer, phone, and a few chairs. On the desk lay a red Cordova leather ledger with the number 368 etched into its cover.

"You would have been—you will be asked to sign out after your visit," *Señora* Melia said. "Every client must."

"This isn't a secure system," I said, looking at the log book.

"It has served us well for a long time. I assure you, the vault was not broken into."

I was tired of hearing that. "You have no idea if that is the case. From where I stand, it seems the people here, at this facility, are the prime suspects. Past and present."

I could see she took offense at the accusation. But we were at a standstill. Nothing this woman could say would absolve the Repository. The matter would need a thorough investigation.

"I'm calling Interpol," I said.

"That is not allowed," the curator said.

"You're kidding, right?"

I was beginning to sound like Cotton, since that's exactly what he would have said.

"The agreement your father signed expressly forbids law enforcement from having access here. It would defeat the purpose of this place if the vaults were subject to official search. The owners of this facility pride themselves on providing supreme customer service, all of which centers around absolute privacy. *Señora* Fortuna, *Señorita* Vitt, truly I feel for you. This is a great mystery and I want to help you learn everything you can. But please believe me, this facility was not involved."

"Your assurance is no comfort," I said, my anger rising. "And let's be realistic. This place is about more than safekeeping. I can only imagine how many tax laws have been broken by your clients in keeping their valuables here. How many treasures do you hold that were acquired illegally? How much stolen property is hidden away here? Maybe some of the world's greatest missing pieces of art? And even if you had a previous incident of something missing, no one would have ever learned of that since, after all, that would make your services a bit…suspect?"

She ignored my new accusations and in a low, even tone said, "We could not survive…if a robbery occurred here."

Finally, a truth.

I opened the ledger.

Esmerelda and I scanned through its pages looking at the dates that my father had visited. Over forty-five times within an eighteen-year period before he died.

"There were only fifteen paintings," I said. "Why do you think he kept coming and going?"

Esmerelda shook her head. "That is impossible to say. There could have been more in that vault then."

True.

"And look." I pointed. "He never spent longer than a few minutes each time. My father could sit in front of a painting for an hour and never move. His visits here, though, were in and out. Quick."

As Cotton would say, *time to turn on the vacuum cleaner and see what gets sucked in.*

"Did you know my father, *Señora* Melia?" I asked.

"No. I have been working here only for the last nine years."

"I still need the owner or owners' names."

"I cannot divulge that information."

"I will find out," I made clear. "And it won't take me long." I pointed to the ledger. "I will need a copy of those pages. Since they concern only my vault, there should not be a problem."

"There is none. I will have a copy made."

"Of every page."

She picked up the phone on the desk and spoke quickly. Less than a minute later a young man arrived and she gave him instructions on making the copy. While he was gone I kept the mental vacuum cleaner on and probed more about the security of the Repository. She answered each one of my inquiries with assurance. The location was secure. The system was regularly maintained. No one who worked there had ever been fired under suspicious circumstances. Security had never been breached.

"And yet, *Señor* Vitt's entire collection is gone," Esmerelda said.

I almost felt sorry for *Señora* Melia. After all, it was entirely possible that the theft occurred between the last time my father visited the vault and her coming to work here. She might be totally in the dark. My money was on an inside job, orchestrated and carried out by people who worked for this so-called impenetrable place.

"When was the last time another vault holder has been down here and checked on his or her belongings?" Esmerelda asked. "Especially one of the vaults not visited all that frequently."

"You know I cannot answer that."

I could read Esmerelda's thoughts. If my father's vault had been compromised, then how many others might have fallen victim too?

Señora Melia seemed to get the point too. "Please allow me the opportunity to conduct an internal investigation. Before you go to the authorities."

"My father trusted your vaults with his most valuable possessions in the world. And this repository let him down. Why should I care about the reputation of this institution?"

"Because," she said, her fear gone, replaced with a surprising resolve, "your father's reputation is tied with ours. Are you familiar with how he purchased each painting? And from what seller? Is everything in order? Perhaps the originals are gone for a reason? One your father sanctioned? You were correct a moment ago. I have learned that not everything in this vault falls into the category of…legitimate."

"I don't like your implications."

The curator stood her ground. "I don't like yours."

"My father was not capable of breaking the law."

"Perhaps not, but, as you both have reminded me more than once, the paintings are still gone."

Chapter 10

ON THE DRIVE BACK TO THE JET, NEITHER ESMERELDA NOR I SPOKE.

I was baffled by the discovery at the Repository and bursting with questions. The damn windows remained fogged the entire way. Which only fueled my rage. All those precautions, yet the employees had *carte blanche* to do whatever they wanted.

That place was anything but secure.

Once we were on board and on our way back to Barcelona, thanks to the privacy that tens of thousands of meters in the air provided, we were able to explore all of the possibilities. Some assumed *Señora* Melia was telling the truth. Others not so much. Esmerelda had been particularly irate, even raising her voice a few times, which was unusual.

"Do you think my father broke any laws in acquiring those paintings?" I asked. "I was a young girl when all that happened. But you were there."

"Many Andorran shell corporations are used for illegal purposes. It's part of the country's allure. Some of those include fraud, tax avoidance, and evading international sanctions. I suspect that's one reason why the Repository is located there. But to my knowledge, Cassiopeia, your father engaged in none of those activities."

"Was he doing anything illegal by bringing his paintings there?"

"That would depend on how and from whom he purchased them. I have no idea of any of that. He did not consult with me. And though I have all of the records, I have never read the provenance on the paintings. But even if they were purchased legally, and if there were tax ramifications to his purchases and he didn't properly report them to the government, then, yes, that would be a crime."

I was puzzled. "What ramifications? What would a buyer of art need to report?"

"Buyers and sellers often enter into agreements to defraud the government and report the sale of a painting for far less than it actually sold for. The seller gives the buyer incentivized discounts in order to keep the money between them. This becomes quite important with estate taxes. And then there is the issue of your father using a free port to store the paintings. Many people who take advantage of countries, like Andorra, to store valuables are engaged in money laundering and tax evasion. But your father could not have been involved in any of that. It was not his nature."

Nor was it consistent with his LDS beliefs.

Which he had taken most seriously.

"He was the paragon of conscientiousness," Esmerelda said. "He would never risk his reputation on doing anything illegal. He had more money than he could ever spend."

"Yet he secreted away his entire art collection and told no one but his lawyer. Who is bound by confidentiality. Did you ever ask him why he moved the collection to Andorra instead of a vault in Spain? If he didn't want to insure the originals, and simply keep them safe, why did he have to take them out of the country to a super-secret repository?"

"It was not my place to question him. But, if I had, I would have simply received one of his looks. And you know what those mean."

I did, recalling how steely his eyes became when filled with anger or annoyance. Whenever I saw that look I headed in the opposite direction. Luckily, it had been rare, and usually business related.

But once it had been directed straight at me.

My senior year in secondary school. My parents were away on a trip, so I invited some friends over. We spent the afternoon swimming and sailing, then grilled food on the beach. Angelina and Paulo had wanted to do all the cooking, but I insisted on handling things myself. Part of my teenage independent streak. We ate steaks, shrimp, potatoes, and fresh bread. Before the party started I visited the wine cellar and brought out a few bottles of Bordeaux to make pitchers of sangria.

The party was a grand success.

No incidents.

Everything was fine.

Until a week later when my father called me into his study and asked why I hadn't allowed Paulo and Angelina to help. He explained he wasn't questioning the gathering, just my refusal to allow our housekeeper and her husband to do their job. I argued that I was old enough to deal with things.

"Apparently not," he'd said. *"You owe me two thousand euros."*

I was shocked. How?

"In your haste to handle everything, you selected the wine from the wrong side of the cellar." I could not believe what he was saying. *"You opened a hundred-year-old bottle, that I purchased at auction, to mix with orange juice and peach slices."*

My parents did not drink alcohol. Not ever. All part of their LDS beliefs. But my father kept the wine for guests and family who did partake. This was at the beginning of my organized rebellion against the Book of Mormon.

So I drank alcohol and caffeine.

I could still see his eyes boring into me.

With disappointment.

That hurt more than I ever wanted to admit.

But I eventually made him proud. I worked at a local café for several months and paid him back every euro I owed. Never would it be said that I took advantage of him.

And never would he do that to me.

I hoped.

I dropped Esmerelda off at her apartment and returned to the villa. Safe inside my room, I called Cotton. I needed help processing. Men, by and large, were fixers. They liked to make things right. Probably goes back to the caveman days when they were hunter-gatherers or some other nonsense. Sometimes, though, all we needed was a listener. And Cotton was good at that. The paintings were once in the vault and now they were gone. How? *Señora* Melia insisted they'd not been stolen. No way to infiltrate the sacred Repository. But I'd learned from bitter experience that if you were faced with something that appeared impossible, it just meant you were not looking at all of the possibilities.

Cotton didn't answer my call.

I left a message.

Short and to the point, but not all that revealing.

Ten minutes later he texted.

In transit. Hope it can wait till tomorrow. Miss you.

I texted back that it could.

Except it couldn't.

I called Miguel and asked if he was free for dinner. He said that he was and agreed to come to the villa. I walked down to the kitchen and asked Angelina if she could stretch the dinner she'd made for one so as to feed two.

Of course, she said.

Angelina always made things happen.

Miguel arrived a half hour later and I brought him into the main parlor. Angelina had laid out a bowl of salted almonds and a plate of glistening green olives. I asked if wine was okay, or if he preferred something else.

He said wine would be good.

"I need some help," I told him, as I poured us each a glass. "Have you ever heard about my father's art collection from people other than me? Someone at the Prado?"

"Of course. One of our longtime directors, Juan Segovia, knew your father. But he's only spoken of the paintings in the most general of terms."

"He never saw the collection?"

"Your father showed him photographs over the years of works he was considering buying. But he never asked Juan to accompany him to an auction or gallery, or meet with any of his dealers, as many other collectors do routinely. Juan told me that your father had promised him that, one day, he'd bring him here but—" Miguel shrugged. "That day never arrived."

"Do you know about a place in Andorra called the Repository?" I asked, getting to the point.

"I do. There are rumors it holds masterpieces that no one will ever see again. Some stolen. Or bought illegally and hidden away."

My fear exactly.

During World War II the Nazis stole art on an industrial scale, most of it from Jews. What they didn't hang in their homes, they hid away in caves and mines and storage facilities in Germany and Austria. After the war, many legitimate collectors and reputable art institutions unknowingly, and some illegitimate collectors knowingly, bought some of that bounty. Records were not kept back then the way we keep them now. No centralized databases, computers, or Internet existed. It was all ledgers and paper files, which could be lost, destroyed, or easily forged. Nor was anyone sensitized to the issue of stolen art. Eventually, hundreds of thousands of pieces had been returned to their rightful owners, or identified and held officially until the rightful owners could be found. But hundreds of thousands more pieces were still missing.

"Is the Repository linked to Nazi plunder?" I asked.

"I have no idea. I have merely heard rumors. I know precious little about the place."

"I was inside it today."

He looked shocked.

"My father had the copies you saw made and placed the originals there for safe keeping."

"So you found them."

"Not exactly." I explained what Esmerelda and I didn't find. "I want to find those paintings." I paused. "I *have* to find them."

"How can I help?"

"You tell me. What do I do? Where do I start?"

"Any documentation of provenance will help. Your father must have kept something? Any literature, exhibition history, receipts, confirmation from the artist's estate, the name of the seller, photos of stamps or marks on the works themselves. They would have all been included with any insurance policy."

"His insurance seems to have been the Repository."

He shook his head in frustration. "That's not good."

I agreed.

"I have to prove to myself that my father didn't buy illegal art. That he wasn't hiding stolen paintings."

"I understand."

"What I really want to know is who owns that repository. I could not discover that today. Can you find out?"

A smile came to his lips.

"That I might be able to do."

Chapter 11

MIGUEL PHONED THE FOLLOWING MORNING TO SAY THAT HE HAD talked to several of the board members for the Prado and one did, in fact, know who owned the Repository. Even better, that person was willing to provide the information, but only in person, face to face. A meeting was set up in the garden at the museum, and Miguel was waiting for me when I arrived. Fifteen minutes later a diminutive woman, aided by a cane, approached. Miguel introduced her as Carmelo Basco, a collector and philanthropist, who told me that we had a connection.

"I knew your father. We served once on a board of directors together. Which is why I was surprised to hear you wanted to connect with the Repository's owner. I don't expect Arturo would be happy for you to have dealings with this man."

"Why do you say that?"

"He's not a reputable figure. He lives and works in the shadowland of the world of art and finance."

"Yet he owns this mysterious Repository, that so many take advantage of. Including my father."

"That is true. But people may do things out of character…when necessary."

My spine stiffened. "What does that mean?"

"Only that do you really know everything about your father?"

"I know that he would have never done anything illegal."

Her silence seemed more irritating than any comeback. Then she reached out and took my hand. Her skin was surprisingly soft despite the arthritic fingers and age spots. "I want you to be careful. Your father would be so angry with me if I led his daughter into danger."

"Were you that close with him?"

"He was, for many years, my bishop. I was his counselor."

That grabbed my attention.

The Church of Jesus Christ of Latter-Day Saints was organized across the globe into congregations. The larger ones were called wards, led by a bishop chosen by the Church hierarchy. The bishop watched over the ward members, guiding them, overseeing teaching, missionary work, and all spiritual growth. He counseled members and administered Church discipline. He cared for the poor and managed all finances and records. A bishop was assisted by two counselors. Now I knew why this woman was no stranger. She'd shared something that a father and daughter had not.

God.

"I can handle myself," I told her. "You don't need to worry. Now, could you please tell me what I want to know?"

"May I ask why it is important you connect with the Repository's owner?"

I looked over at Miguel.

"I told her nothing," he said.

Prudence cautioned that as few people as possible should know what had happened to my father's art collection. If it had been stolen, Interpol would have a better chance conducting an investigation if things were kept close. Once word got out, it might send the thief even deeper to ground. Stolen art was hard enough to find under the best circumstances.

And these were anything but best.

I knew little to nothing about the old dowager standing before me, and her references to my father could be a way to drop my guard. Miguel had told me that he too was unfamiliar with her, and that he was working off an introduction made by one of his board members. What if she was connected to the man who owned the Repository? Acting as a spy. Trying to find out what she could. Or was she a lure? Here to draw me in further. Was I being paranoid? Maybe.

But understandably so.

"It's not important that you know why," I said. "Either tell me his name, or let's end this conversation."

"You are so much like him," she said. "Strong-willed. Determined. Fearless."

"Thank you."

And I meant it.

"The man who owns the Repository is Robert Travers."

Never heard of him. "Where do I find him?"

"He is a man without a country. He lives on a yacht and spends his time in international waters."

"He sounds afraid."

"He has good reason to be. As I said, his reputation is not one of an honest man."

"Yet rich people seem to trust him enough to secret away their valuables in his Repository."

"He's forged a reputation of being able to offer that service. Strangely, many have trusted him. I being one of those."

"You have a vault there?"

The old woman nodded. "For a long time."

"Have you checked it lately?" I asked.

She shook her head.

"I would, if I were you. Robert Travers may not be as trustworthy as he wants people to think."

Finding Travers turned out to be easy.

I first made inquiries with Terra's corporate headquarters in Paris. Its resources were global and it took only an hour for a call to come back saying where I could locate the man. An hour after that Miguel and I climbed aboard the corporate jet and headed out over the Mediterranean to the Spanish island of Ibiza. I'd asked him to come along to deal with any art issues that might arise. He was far more knowledgeable on that subject than I was.

Ibiza sat about a hundred and fifty kilometers off the coast from Valencia. A rocky spit, about six times smaller than Majorca, but ten times larger than Manhattan. Famous for its nightlife and dance halls, its tourism board had, of late, tried to bill it as more family friendly. Hard to know if that effort had borne any fruit, since I'd never visited. It was also a World Heritage Site, which caused me to smile. Cotton and I both had a bad history with those. Not that we intentionally set out to cause any damage, it just seemed to work out that way.

The flight was short and, once on the ground, we took a taxi to the yacht club, which occupied a choice spot on the southern shore. My people at corporate headquarters had learned that Travers was anchored about fifty nautical kilometers off Ibiza, in, you guessed it, international waters. I had already hired by phone a boat and captain, which was waiting for us. We hopped aboard and headed off onto the blue Mediterranean.

The ride was smooth and uneventful.

I'd always loved the sea. I grew up beside it and learned to sail at an early age. One of the benefits of being born to privilege was the ability to savor so many diverse things. And I'd definitely partaken. Sailing, rock climbing, spelunking, scuba diving, motorcycles, fast cars.

I'd tried them all.

And the older I got the more risk I seemed to want to take. Though my thrills these days were confined to the adventures I seemed to find myself experiencing more often than not. Having an ex-Justice Department intelligence agent as a boyfriend certainly afforded lots of opportunities.

And I'd not turned a single one down.

Nor would I. I liked living on the edge.

And I loved sharing those experiences with Cotton.

There was no way to announce our visit in advance, which was probably a good thing. Miguel was concerned that Travers would not meet with us. But I didn't think that was going to be a problem.

In fact, I was fairly certain he was expecting us.

The weather was perfect. Clear skies. Calm seas. Temperature in the mid-twenties Celsius. I'd worn jeans, a cotton shirt, and a light jacket, which also allowed me to come armed. A nine-millimeter semiautomatic rested tight to my spine. I hoped it would not be required, but it was good to be prepared.

Travers' boat came into view.

Excuse me. Not a boat. More like a small cruise liner pretending to be a yacht. It was sleek and stylish. Like a spaceship. With a striking white hull, lots of shiny glass windows, and what looked like a helicopter pad toward its bow.

"That's a hundred meters long," Miguel said.

"More like one-fifty."

Painted to its stern was a name.

Sanctuaire.

Sanctuary.

I smiled. At least Travers had a sense of humor.

We motored up alongside, met by a man on the upper deck wielding an automatic rifle who asked our business.

"I want to speak with Robert Travers," I called out.

"He takes no visitors. Especially unannounced."

And the man gestured with the rifle that we should leave.

"Tell him I am the daughter of Arturo Pedro Cristóbal Vitt and I have come to speak to him about my father's paintings. He's expecting me."

I was counting on *Señora* Melia from the Repository to have immediately contacted her employer and reported the problem.

The man with the rifle never moved.

"Tell him," I added, "that we can either speak now, or Interpol will be visiting his facility in Andorra before nightfall."

The man continued to hesitate, as if not wanting to be an errand boy.

I shrugged. "All right. I tried. Let's go."

And I motioned for the boat's captain to take us away.

The engines revved and we were about to leave when a shot rang out.

I motioned for the captain to return the engines to neutral. The sentry had fired into the air to garner our attention.

Which worked.

"*Señor* Travers will see you," the man called out.

Chapter 12

MIGUEL AND I STEPPED ABOARD.

Everything about the ship screamed obscene money and power.

A mid-20th century style dominated. Pared-back. Curvaceous. Nostalgic. Everything an array of flowing shapes and vintage lamps. None of the wood veneers that were once popular, like glossy teak or shiny mahogany, could be seen. Here everything was a textural timber, lots of beech, birch, and pine, which brought an even more contemporary feel. The floors looked like gnarled oak, a wood I loved, one with character, expensive too. I stole a few glances into a large saloon outfitted with plush, comfortable furniture and works of art on the walls. A huge rug covered the floor, its colors fading from aquamarine to white, like waves lapping at a powdered beach. I noticed that its texture seemed interactive, the effect enhanced by the footprints that pushed the threads this way and that, like the chop of the ocean.

The armed steward led us to a staircase that wound down into the bowels of the yacht. At the end of a short corridor we entered a small room. One wall, clearly at the yacht's stern, was a half-submerged window that provided a spectacular underwater view. I assumed there was plenty of tech behind that feat. The glass, or whatever material it was, seemed several centimeters thick and double paned. Amphitheatre seating rose away from the window that would accommodate ten people. A deep blue carpet tossed off more of a watery feel. Dark wood framed out the spectacular view.

A man stood before the window.

Handsome. Beefy, but with muscle not fat. He had a full head of wavy silver hair and curious dark eyes. *Señora* Basco had said Travers would be nearing eighty, but the man standing before us looked a good two decades younger. A thick gold chain hung around his neck and a diamond Franck Muller watch wrapped his right wrist. His pressed white slacks, white shirt and blue deck shoes matched the yacht's color scheme.

"I am Robert Travers," he said. "I assume you are Cassiopeia Vitt, the sole owner of Terra. And you are Miguel Velez, of the Prado museum."

Good. He *was* expecting us.

"What do you think of my Nemo room?" he asked.

I caught the reference to *20,000 Leagues Under the Sea.* I'd loved that Disney movie.

"There are countless regulations that restrict what you can do above and beneath the waterline." He pointed out to the ocean. "But not a one for halfway between."

He seemed proud of that loophole.

"It took two years to get this approved. But when I sit here and watch the sea pass by, it's worth every bit of the trouble."

He was posturing, so I let him.

"How about some coffee, tea, water?" he asked.

I decided to do a little posturing of my own. "Tea would be fine." I glanced at Miguel. "For us both."

Travers motioned to the man with the rifle and a steward appeared with three cups of tea, a plate of mini croissants and *pain au* chocolate, along with a bowl of gleaming grapes and strawberries. The china was monogramed with the boat's name, as were the linen napkins. Of course. What else would they have? Neither I nor Miguel partook of the refreshments. Travers ignored them too.

"Interesting name you gave this boat," I said.

"This is, indeed, my sanctuary."

"What are you afraid of?" Miguel asked.

Travers spread his arms out in a mock embrace. "What's not to be afraid of? Government. Big business. The media. All of them are nothing but trouble. Here? On this sanctuary, safe in international waters, I rule supreme."

On the flight from Barcelona, I'd checked out Travers online. The Terra corporate jet came equipped with a state-of-the-art communications system. But the information was sparse and incomplete. So I'd placed a call to a friend, Pierre Marcher, a former police inspector who'd helped me out a while back with some problems that arose in Paris. Luckily, we were able to connect and he told me all about Robert Travers.

He was an Irishman, born near Cork on the southwest coast, who made a fortune shipping durable goods to Africa and the Middle East. Eventually, he metamorphized those trade routes into *legal* arms dealing. He supposedly began his career in the 1970s, brokering deals between American arms manufacturers and the Saudi Arabian government. Lockheed Martin reportedly paid him over a hundred million dollars in commissions for those sales. He'd also worked with other American, French, and Israeli corporations to broker deals. He'd even acquired a nickname. The Leprechaun. His company, Viking Traders, a Luxembourg entity, had long dealt in global weaponry, including small arms, tanks, fighter planes, even ballistic missiles.

And all of it legal.

Africa had become a big market for him of late.

He was the quintessential middleman, negotiating deals that allowed buyers and sellers a high degree of anonymity.

Making him a lot of money.

Enough to buy this cruise liner of a yacht.

Supposedly, he'd once been the foremost seller of weapons to Saddam Hussein during the 1980s. With the full knowledge and backing of the CIA, Travers sold arms to Iraq in the midst of the Iran-Iraq war. He also sold weaponry to militia groups during the Lebanese civil war, as well as to Ecuador and Nicaragua, and to Argentina during the Falklands War. Following the first Gulf War, he'd finally shown his true colors when he was accused of selling arms to Iraq, but he escaped United States prosecution, leading many to believe he'd been working both sides of the sale.

"How long have you owned the Repository?" I asked.

"I created it forty years ago. To satisfy a need I found among the world's rich. People like your father, who I knew by the way."

Which disgusted me. "What was his need?"

Travers pointed. "The same as many. He possessed some marvelous paintings that he wanted to keep safe."

"You saw them?"

Travers shook his head. "I was not so lucky. But when he applied for membership he told me about them. It is a requirement. We need to know what's going in those vaults. Can't have anything illegal or dangerous there."

"How utterly decent of you," I said. "My paintings are gone."

"That remains to be seen. Our records indicate that your vault has not been opened since the last time your father visited."

"I have little confidence in your records," I said.

"*Señora* Melia told me about your accusations. That someone at the Repository may have breached your father's vault. That's ridiculous. We have never had an incident. Never. Not once."

"I'm tired of hearing that. What I'm waiting to hear is what you plan to do about mine."

"Not a thing."

No surprise there.

"Then I will involve Interpol," I said. "This entire matter should be a criminal investigation anyway."

"Are you sure?" Travers asked.

I did not like his cavalier tone.

"*Mademoiselle* Vitt, you have to ask yourself a hard question—"

"Why the French label?" I interrupted and asked.

"Oh, come now. I know you live in Givors and are building a castle. How exciting that must be." He'd obviously prepared for this visit. And seemed proud of the fact. "You must tell me about it sometime."

Like that was going to happen.

"As I was saying, you have to ask yourself, why did your father choose to use the Repository to store his originals? I'm sure he offered the excuse that he did not want to shoulder the insurance and security costs. And there is truth to that. But, as you may or may not know, nothing in the Repository is insured. There's no need. It's merely a secret location with extraordinary security. The clients who choose to lease a vault understand that. Yes, they are taking a chance with valuable assets. But they are willing to take that chance. In fact, they pay me large sums of money in order to take that chance. Why would they do such a foolish thing?" Travers paused. "They take the chance because they have to. What they place inside my vaults is not something they want the world to see. They want it hidden away, where only they have access. So, *Mademoiselle* Vitt, what was your father hiding? Perhaps Interpol can find that out."

I got the message. Loud and clear. This was a two-edged sword. And the bastard was right. So I made a decision.

I'd handle the investigation myself.

I also realized this had been a waste of time.

"We're done."

And I motioned for Miguel to leave.

"I'm so glad you dropped by," Travers said. "Do come again. Perhaps under more pleasant circumstances."

I kept my temper and held my tongue.

Travers led the way up the stairs, back to the main deck and the large salon. "*Señor* Velez, you might find my collection that I have on board of interest. I switch out the paintings a few times a year. Right now, I have an impressionist theme on display."

Four framed paintings decorated the salon.

"Sisley, of course," Travers said, pointing to a harbor scene of St. Tropez, where I knew the painter had spent most of his life.

Next Travers pointed to an image of the French port of Le Havre. The early morning blues, lavenders, and grays were lovely.

"Monet," he said.

Travers pointed to a far wall. "A favorite Winslow Homer."

Neither Miguel nor I needed help with the attribution. The rough seas and adrift boat couldn't have been captured that way by any other artist.

"And lastly"—our host gestured to a fourth painting—"one of Matisse's most charming views of Nice harbor. The Bay of Angels."

I nodded, as I enjoyed the composition of the water viewed through a pair of lovely French windows, their curtains blowing in the breeze.

Miguel stepped closer to the paintings and admired them.

He stepped back.

Then close again.

Exactly as he'd done when he inspected my father's paintings.

"They're fakes," Miguel said. "Excellent copies. But still copies."

Travers smiled. "Of course. Why would I display the originals? Nearly no one, other than a trained eye like yours, would know the difference. These are some excellent copies."

I said nothing, realizing that he'd wanted Miguel to make the observation.

"But I have copies because I live on a boat," Travers said. "Why did *Señor* Vitt see the need for such measures? It seems a mystery."

His eyes bore into me.

"Perhaps one the authorities can solve."

I said nothing.

Instead, Miguel and I headed for the exit.

"*Mademoiselle* Vitt."

I stopped and turned back. All civility had fled the older face.

"I do hope this is the last time I hear from you."

I had no intention of being intimidated.

"Don't count on it."

Chapter 13

THE NEXT NIGHT I HAD DINNER WITH JOCASTA. WE WENT TO A popular spot, La Rocca de Tossa, right on the beach, a place we'd frequented since we were girls.

Travers' final threat still rang in my ears.

I do hope this is the last time I hear from you.

He knew that I would not involve the police. But what he did not know was that I was more than capable of handling things on my own. I also had backup. Cotton Malone. Who I could call in at any time. Together we'd faced a lot.

And we could face this too.

But, for now, I opted to keep this a solo project.

Castelldefels lay about twenty minutes south of Barcelona on the main train line. It sat along a wide sandy beach lined with bustling restaurants and lively bars, most with outdoor seating where drinks and food could be enjoyed. The town had a low-key vibe, always blessed with a mild climate, even in winter. We ordered our regular sangria and the paella, the restaurant's signature dish. While we ate I filled her in on what happened on Travers' yacht.

"Do you seriously think your father was engaged in something improper?" she asked.

I considered the question carefully. Finally, I said, "To be honest, all of this is really strange. There are so many unanswered questions."

At least I'd managed to learn more about Travers.

He'd always been something of a playboy. A Wikipedia page, not all that authoritative, indicated four marriages and some questionable relationships with young women. Two had resulted in lawsuits, but nothing was noted as to their outcome. Rumors abounded that he might be involved in human trafficking. But, again, nothing had ever risen above rumor and innuendo. Certainly a man with Travers' reputation would attract trouble. He probably thrived on it. And nobody bought a boat the size of a destroyer and avoided every country's territorial waters for no reason. But the Repository? That opened Travers up to scrutiny and liability. So why have it? I didn't know the answer to that question, but I intended to find out.

Having my parents die within a year of each other, during a period when we remained semi-estranged, had left me with more than grief. Instead, a deep regret had settled over me for some time. A plague of the what-ifs. What had Longfellow said? *Let the past bury its dead.* Easier said than done.

I became aware that Jocasta had taken my hand in hers.

She knew me well enough to read my thoughts.

"You're going to solve this," she said. "You're going to find the answers."

I appreciated her resolve.

It helped.

The waiter arrived and removed our plates. We both declined the dessert menu and told him we'd just finish the wine. Which we did, switching the conversation to the new man in Jocasta's life. Since her divorce, she'd been serially dating, no one special, but, according to her, this one might be different.

"Out of the frying pan and into the platter?" I asked with a smile.

"Let's hope not."

I agreed. She deserved happiness.

The waiter brought the check, which we paid, then left the restaurant. The crowds were still going strong, the night young. Castelldefels had a lovely pedestrian-only area that stretched along part of the waterfront which drew people from all around. I'd enjoyed many a walk here. Some alone, some with suitors, some with old friends.

But never with my parents.

They were like that. There, but not there. Warm, but cold. I could recall few hugs from either of them, though I knew they both loved me. I always downplayed the lack of emotion and made excuses about it. But I never realized how their aloofness affected me until they were both gone.

I missed them.

And I'd like to think they missed me too.

We made our way down the cobblestones, enjoying the warm evening and the steady ocean breeze. Suddenly, about fifty meters away, a car entered the restricted zone. It happened from time to time as the merchants required deliveries to their establishments.

But always during the day.

Never at night.

It immediately doused its headlights, eased its way down the wide promenade, and stopped. People threw it a few looks, but otherwise ignored it.

The driver's side door opened and a man rolled out.

He then fled on foot in the opposite direction.

Alarm bells rose in my head.

Was this an attack?

A car bomb?

"Everyone," I called out. "Run. Now. Away from that car."

Jocasta stared at me in disbelief. Surely both at my words and the threat. I took my own advice and grabbed her arm, leading her away.

We started to run.

The pedestrian-only zone ended about ten meters ahead. Beyond was a busy boulevard which, during the day, churned with traffic. In the evening cars were there, only fewer and far between. I glanced back. People were still fleeing the parked car, which now sat alone.

My adrenaline flowed.

I turned back to face Jocasta and the street beyond.

My gaze raked the scene. My car was parked twenty meters away down the sidewalk. I'd managed to snag a choice spot earlier as someone was leaving when I arrived. Nothing had happened with the car behind us and we were now a long way from it.

My senses were on high alert.

Jocasta seemed flustered, but otherwise okay.

Then I saw it.

A black four-door coupe. Cruising down the boulevard. Headed our way. And while the other traffic was moving along, this car was slowing.

Its rear window lowered.

I caught the gleam of a rifle barrel as the car came close to parallel with us. Reacting, I grabbed Jocasta's arm and dragged us both down to the concrete sidewalk, landing behind a parked BMW.

Gunfire erupted.

The BMW's windows shattered under the hail of rounds. More

bullets thudded into the steel on the other side.

A tire exploded.

I reached back and grabbed my weapon, which I'd kept on me since earlier on the trip to Travers' yacht.

"Stay down," I told Jocasta.

Then I headed for the BMW's rear end and rose up, sending three well-placed rounds into the attacking car's rear window.

Tires squealed.

The dark coupe sped away.

I kept the gun aimed, but the car was gone, out of range.

I rushed over to Jocasta. "Are you all right?"

She was shaking, but nodded. "You came armed?"

No time to explain. "We need to get out of here."

Clearly the parked car back in the pedestrian-only area had been designed to flush us this way. The other vehicle had timed its approach perfectly. What they'd not counted on was that, as Cotton would say, *this was not my first rodeo.*

I was glad Jocasta was okay.

"You're tough," my old friend said.

"It's nothing new."

"You're going to have to tell me about that sometime."

I tossed her a smile. "Maybe."

"You do realize that somebody just tried to kill us," she said. "But who?"

The answer to her question seemed not in doubt.

We both found our cars.

I insisted Jocasta come back to the villa where I could keep an eye on her. She'd been pretty shaken by the attack. Which I could understand. Getting shot at was no fun. Nothing about it was good. Nothing about it was not upsetting. The trick was to control your emotions and steady your nerves. I'd undergone several trainings, one at an elite academy in Austria where personal bodyguards were groomed. I'd learned a lot there. How to shoot, how to drive a car under pressure, how to watch, observe, and sense trouble. But I'd also learned even more in the field by doing things.

Before I sped away and headed for the villa, I had to make sure that Miguel was okay. He'd gone with me to Travers. So I dialed his cell phone. He answered and I told him what happened.

"I'm home, and everything is fine here," he said.

I wasn't comforted, but there was nothing I could do. I had precious little in the way of proof as to much of anything, though I knew Travers was the culprit.

Who else could it be?

"Watch yourself," I told him. "And let's meet in the morning."

"I'm looking into some things. I'll be at my office by eleven."

Chapter 14

I ARRIVED AT THE PRADO AT 10:45 A.M.

Crossing the lobby of one of the greatest art institutions in the world, I felt the stirrings of awe that always rose inside me when I visited museums. Elegant buildings filled with timeless treasures soothed me. The Metropolitan in New York. The Louvre in Paris. The Uffizi in Florence. So many grand spaces. I felt at home as soon as I stepped into a museum, surrounded by centuries of what talented human beings had created. Sometimes for function. Other times out of compulsion. Most simply for beauty's sake. It always restored my faith in humankind. Nations that voluntarily destroyed their art and culture were not only the lesser for it, they were doomed.

No exceptions.

As Cotton always said, *history matters*.

I left the public spaces and reached the glass doors that led to the inner sanctum. Here were the offices of the curators, restorers, the library, and the elevators to the storage facility that lay below ground. Like many museums around the world, the Prado owned far more than what could ever be displayed at any one time.

A receptionist looked up as I approached.

She was in her twenties, wearing a stylish red suit. A simple gold cross lay in the hollow of her neck. Her eyes were red-rimmed.

She'd been crying.

"Are you okay?" I asked.

She shook her head.

"What's wrong."

"It's *Señor* Velez. He was in an accident."

I drove straight to Barcelona and rushed into the hospital.

What I learned was that Miguel had been coming to work on his scooter, like every day when it wasn't raining, and was swiped by a car. He'd been thrown from the scooter and, thankfully, he'd found the grassy shoulder instead of hard asphalt. He'd also been wearing a helmet. The offending vehicle had kept going. The police had told the museum that witnesses varied in their recollections, but one fact had been consistent.

A dark, four-door coupe.

That was no coincidence.

I found Miguel in a room on the eighth floor, his wife by his bedside. His head was bandaged, a cast on his right leg, but he was awake and smiling as I entered.

"Are you okay?"

"I think I'll live," he said.

His wife's face was a mass of concern. "I've told him about that scooter. People drive like idiots."

I listened as Miguel explained that he'd been clearly in the bike lane, but the vehicle that hit him had veered over and clipped him from behind. I decided not to say any more about Travers or what had happened to me last night. No need to panic Miguel and his wife any further.

What happened here was a message.

That car could have easily killed my friend.

But it had not.

They missed with the hit in Castelldefels, so they struck as close to home as possible. Telegraphing me *to back off.* I would deal with this. By going straight to the source. But first I spent a half hour visiting with Miguel. His wife seemed to steadily calm down. I needed to get him away from trouble.

And there seemed only one way.

Direct it.

Straight at me.

I left the hospital and, outside, placed a call to Esmerelda, telling her all that had happened during the past twenty-four hours. I heard her sigh when I finished, then she went silent in a moment of contemplation.

"Perhaps it is time to involve the police," she said.

"They would just get in my way. I can handle this."

"Are you sure?"

I realized that my godmother knew little about my extracurricular activities. I'd been involved in some fairly high-stakes exploits. I'd jumped out of airplanes, avoided explosives, been chased in cars and shot at more times than I could remember. I knew how to handle a gun, deal with pressure, and get myself out of trouble. About the only thing that got to me was high places. Not a full-fledged fear of heights, but about as close as one could get. I could always call on Cotton, and even some help from Stephanie Nelle and the Magellan Billet. I also had a close relationship with ex-American president Danny Daniels. Not to mention the many European law enforcement people I'd dealt with. So this was not going to be, like Cotton would say, *amateur hour.*

Far from it.

"I got this," I told Esmerelda.

"I disagree."

Time to pull rank. "Noted. But you're the lawyer and I'm the client. What I need from you is access to my father's papers which, I know, you have in storage. I need to see everything you have on those fifteen paintings. I'll be at your office within an hour."

And I ended the call.

When I arrived at Esmerelda's office she had coffee and churros waiting. If she was angry, or hurt by my shortness on the phone, she did not reveal a thing.

"I know my father bought art all over the world," I said to her. "Most of it, though, was through a dealer in Paris. Lucien Hammerstein. He has a gallery there."

I could tell by her demeanor that this was all business. Like I'd said. She was the lawyer. I was the client. I hated we were at this point, but I could fix things with her later. Right now, I had to deal with the situation, as presented.

On her conference room table sat a thick file binder.

"Those are the records that deal with the paintings," she told me.

I opened the binder and began to peruse the pages. My father had been meticulous about receipts and documentation. I recall him many times speaking about that detail.

Provenance stamps something with significance beyond what it would otherwise appear to have. It's the history of the item. An interesting provenance might tell a story of fortunes made and lost, a succession of owners, and remarkable epochs from its past. Never underestimate it.

I planned to not do just that.

Provenance confirmed the works creation date, its artist, it showed a history, which helped in determining if the piece had ever been altered or was stolen or looted. Things like original receipts, handwritten notes or inscriptions, plaques, sewn-in tags, or notes on backs of paintings, even photographs, often showing the work with its original owner or some other well-known person, were helpful. A complete set of owners and any auction records were good to have too. Even things like a mention in someone's home inventory, or in a will, a diary, or a written account of seeing it mattered. I knew that the quality of provenance affected the value of the art. An expert certification meant the difference between having no value and being worth a fortune. When provenance was determined, a certificate became attached to the work and followed it from owner to owner.

Like a bill of sale for a car.

So I was curious as to what my father had accepted as authoritative at the time of his purchases.

"Is this all that relates to his art?" I asked Esmerelda.

"It's all I have. The most important papers were probably at the Repository with the paintings themselves."

I sighed. "Which means they are gone too."

That meant I had one play left.

Lucien Hammerstein.

In Paris.

Chapter 15

I LEFT ESMERELDA'S OFFICE.

Back at the villa I called the gallery and managed to get Hammerstein himself on the phone. I explained who I was and asked if he'd sold the paintings to my father. He was quite businesslike and told me he couldn't discuss his clients.

My patience ran thin.

Fast.

"I am the daughter of Arturo Pedro Cristóbal Vitt. The sole beneficiary of his estate. *Monsieur* Hammerstein, I am your client."

My assertion worked. He told me that he'd worked with my father for many years and, yes, he'd bought paintings for him. I requested an appointment and he made one for the next day.

I left the villa and headed straight for the airport.

The corporate jet flew me to Orly. I took a cab to a boutique hotel on the Left Bank, housed in a lovely 1926 building just off St. Germain des Prés. I often stayed at the Montalembert not only for its old-world ambiance, but modern functionality. Its underground parking was also an asset, which made it easy for me to be dropped off and picked up without being seen.

I checked in, headed to my room, and ordered a light dinner of an omelet, salad, and a glass of Sancerre from room service. Then I pulled out the binder of documents. There'd been no time to study them until now and I had resisted the urge on the flight. I realized it was only paper, but it represented a tangible connection to my father. One of the last there would be.

I spread out all of the pages.

Lots of bills of sale and information for over a hundred paintings, drawings, and prints bought from several different galleries and auction houses. I decided to separate it into three piles. One for the fifteen masterpieces. One that related to Lucien Hammerstein. The other for all his other works of art. The latter group was the most numerous, followed by about thirty pages that mentioned Hammerstein. But not a document relating to the fifteen missing paintings was there.

I decided to focus on the Hammerstein receipts. Some were specific to pieces that were still displayed at the villa. Others to those that had been sold long ago. A few of the receipts were vague, the descriptions innocuous, the prices paid impressive.

What were these for?

I played a hunch and found the copies of the ledger from the Repository that I'd also brought along. I cross referenced the receipts with the ledger and discovered a visit to the Repository around three months after each receipt. But was the receipt for one of the masterpieces? There were not fifteen. And was three months about how long it took to make a copy?

Nothing within the binder offered up any documentation about the provenance of the fifteen missing paintings.

Not a word.

Why was something so vital gone?

Perhaps Esmerelda was right and that documentation had been stored in the Repository.

It was possible.

I shuffled through the paperwork again, hoping I'd overlooked something.

But no such luck.

Chapter 16

THE HAMMERSTEIN GALLERY WAS LOCATED AT 61 AVENUE BOÉTIE IN the 8th Arrondissement, a mere ten-minute walk from the Arc de Triomphe and the over- crowded Champs-Élysées. About the same distance, in the opposite direction, to Parc Monceau—my favorite Parisian green space.

I had Terra's front office arrange my transportation and a car was waiting for me in the underground lot. For safety's sake we took a circuitous route to my appointment to make sure no one was following.

I stepped from the car in front of a Beaux-Arts, late 19th century building that featured ornate wooden doors and beautiful iron grillwork. Inside I walked up the marble staircase to the first floor. The Hammerstein wasn't a street-level gallery that welcomed art lovers just browsing. Visits were by appointment only.

I rang the doorbell.

A chic young woman dressed in black, with a Hermès scarf wrapped around her neck, ushered me inside. The foyer was bereft of art, with light gray walls and glossy white molding. Double height windows were graced with sheer white drapes that allowed daylight to creep in. Stainless furniture accentuated the elegant 19th century architecture, creating a sleek, soothing atmosphere. I'd seen the combination many times before, that peculiar French mix of old and new.

She offered me a seat and asked if I'd care for an espresso, which I accepted. Not because I was thirsty. More to root myself in. She returned with a tiny china cup and saucer on a tray which she placed on a side table comprised of three glass circles secured by a steel rod base.

Odd. But interesting.

Monsieur Hammerstein kept me waiting fifteen minutes.

Finally, a man in his mid-sixties, medium height, slim, and wearing a slightly rumpled navy suit emerged from behind a closed door, apologizing profusely. He took my hand, kissed it, and ushered me into his office, which was decorated in much the same manner as the reception area. His desk was a glass and tubular steel concoction, with an oversized black leather chair. A wall of books rose behind it. Facing the desk stretched a long, rectangular glass table with six more leather chairs. Floor to ceiling windows were framed by gray tweed curtains, draped back with black silk tassels. Unlike in the outer rooms, this one was filled with art. Framed sketches dotted the walls, floor to ceiling. Maybe a couple of hundred. My trained eye picked out van Gogh, Renoir, Rodin, Klimt, and what might be a da Vinci, and a Rubens. The carefully curated collection could have been a proud part of any museum.

"Your art is amazing," I said.

"My grandfather started the collection."

"It's quite something."

Still looking, I noticed a Dalí and a Matisse.

"*Mademoiselle* Vitt, first let me tell you what a pleasure it is to see you again. I think you were about ten the last time we met."

I nodded. "I remember. But it wasn't here, was it? I don't recognize these offices."

"It was in Nice. We have a small gallery there. Do you still have the roses?" he asked, referring to the small Renoir oil painting of a vase of roses that my father had bought for me that day.

"I do. In my bedroom south of here, at Givors."

"That's marvelous. I have read about your reconstruction project. How exciting to be building a castle exactly as they did eight hundred years ago. That has to be challenging."

"To say the least."

"And expensive."

"It is. Luckily, I can afford it."

He chuckled. "I'm sure you can. Your father died as one of the wealthiest men in the world. From what I know, you have done nothing but add to that fortune."

He was being charming, which I appreciated. Who didn't like their ego stroked just a little, now and then? "How well did you know my father?"

"Quite well, actually. He was a wonderful man and a great collector. He was older than me, but we were not only client and dealer, we were friends. I enjoyed helping him build his collection."

"That collection is why I am here. I have discovered that some of the paintings hanging in our family villa are forgeries."

"Are you saying we sold—"

I held up my hand. "I'm not accusing you of anything. The discovery led me to learn that my father had copies made of each of those fifteen masterpieces."

Hammerstein visibly relaxed.

"I have further discovered that my father kept his originals in something called the Repository, located in Andorra. Do you know of it?"

"I do. It's a place many have used on occasion. Personally, I have never availed myself of such a service."

"The paintings are gone," I told him. "My father's vault is empty."

Hammerstein rose and approached the window where he stood, his back to me for a few moments. Finally, he turned around. "Robert Travers is a man not to be trusted."

He'd obviously quickly connected all of the dots.

"Why do you say that?"

"Experience. I was unaware that your father had dealings with him. I'm sorry this has happened."

"Has your gallery worked with him? Have you sold him art?"

He waved off my inquiry. "I am not at liberty to either admit or deny that question. But I am heartbroken to learn of the missing paintings. I will do what I can to help you find them."

I shifted tack. "Did my father ever ask you to resell any of his paintings? Perhaps quietly for some reason?"

He shook his head. "Never."

"Did you help him find an artist to copy the paintings?"

"He did not consult with me on that either. Of course, I am aware of the practice of copying paintings, then storing the originals away. It's not uncommon."

"Have you ever had any dealings with Travers?" I asked, this time quickly, watching his face, searching for any reaction.

"As I said, *Mademoiselle* Vitt, I can't discuss that."

"I did not ask if he was a client. I simply asked have you ever dealt with him, outside of this gallery. That's not covered by confidentiality."

He grinned. "Clever, you are. But, still, I cannot discuss Travers. Nor do I particularly want to."

Chapter 17

I'VE LEARNED A LOT FROM COTTON.

He likes to work, as he says, *under the radar*, keeping people off guard, hoping they will underestimate him. But he also liked to quote Einstein. Which I always found a little odd. *Never underestimate your own ignorance.* That was good advice. Especially when the hairs on the back of my neck were quivering, signaling alert.

Like now.

"Let's get back to my father's paintings," I said. "I've gone through his papers and can't find any documentation regarding provenance for his most valuable fifteen canvases. How many of those did you sell to him?"

"All of them."

That was a surprise.

"He trusted me implicitly and relied on my judgment."

"I've found papers and provenance for his lessor paintings, and for my Renoir roses. But nothing for the paintings in question. Do you know why that might be?"

He walked back and sat in his leather chair, leaning back, as if distancing himself from my question. "I have no idea. I can't imagine your father would have destroyed, or lost, that documentation. He was most definitely supplied with the proper papers at the time of purchase. As you know, without it, the validity of those paintings would be in jeopardy."

"Hence why I'm here, asking these questions. Do you have copies of that documentation?"

"That was a long time ago. I'm afraid any copies we might have retained are gone. We had a fire in the warehouse where they were stored about five years ago. We lost a great deal of our vital documentation."

How utterly unfortunate.

And convenient.

Somewhere along the way in my extracurricular activities I'd constructed a set of filters that allowed me to strain through bullshit and condense out the truth. At a minimum, they always warned me when I was being played. At the moment, those filters were working overtime.

Sending out alerts.

I had a bad feeling about Lucien Hammerstein. Nothing about him seemed right. So I decided to do what Cotton liked to do. *Shake the barrel and see what sloshed out.*

"One other thing, *Monsieur* Hammerstein. Since repatriation has become such a serious issue in the last twenty years, is it possible any of my father's paintings might have had…questionable provenance?"

He said nothing.

"My father bought those paintings when reparation first began to become a worldwide concern. So I was wondering if it's possible if any of them might have ownership issues? Is that perhaps why my father kept the collection hidden?"

"Do you know much about the history of our firm?"

A curious reply to my question, but I decided to play along. "Very little."

"If you have a few minutes," he said, "I'd like to show you something."

I nodded. What else did I have to do?

He stepped from his office and returned a couple of minutes later accompanied by a woman wearing a white smock and carrying a leather-bound album.

"*Mademoiselle* Vitt, meet *Madame* Dessou, our in-house restorer. She's also our unofficial historian. I've asked her to bring in a presentation she's been working on for the last two years. We've found many of our clients are interested in learning about our heritage."

Madame Dessou was older than me, maybe in her sixties, a petite woman with a thin, pretty face. Her silver hair was cut in a chin-length bob. Long bangs framed espresso-colored eyes. Her skin was unusually smooth, and her lips were painted in a scarlet red that French women preferred far more than others. Under her white smock she wore stylish black trousers and black suede loafers. She extended a hand and I was surprised by how cold the skin was when we shook. She wasn't wearing any jewelry, save for a small diamond Jewish star hanging in the hollow of her neck.

Hammerstein indicated for us to sit at the conference table.

We did.

I had the impression they'd conducted this performance before.

Madame Dessou laid the album in front of me and opened it to the first page, which displayed a sepia-toned photo of this building, around what looked like the turn of the 20th century.

"This firm was started in 1870 by Abraham Hammerstein," she said. "An important antiques dealer."

The history lesson continued.

In the 1890s, Abraham's two sons, Leo and Victor, began to handle paintings, prints, and sculpture. By 1898 they were known in both Paris and New York as major dealers of Impressionist and Post-Impressionist art. The brothers not only had a great eye for talent, they had money to support struggling artists, becoming their patrons. This helped them create exclusive relationships and build loyalties that led to the gallery becoming one of the most important in Paris. By 1936 Hammerstein was the main dealer for such luminaries as Picasso, Braque, Marie Laurencin, Fernand Léger, and Matisse.

With rumors of war, the brothers, who were Jewish, feared for their lives. So Leo moved to Switzerland and Victor to New York. They left a newly made partner, Alain Blanche, who was not a Jew nor a relation, in Paris to maintain the gallery. Most of the artists the firm handled fell under what Hitler called degenerate art. Their work had been banned from being shipped into Germany, but that didn't mean the Germans underestimated its value.

"All the so-called degenerate art the Nazis looted was kept in Paris at the Galerie Nationale du Jeu de Paume in what insiders called the Martyrs Room."

Madame Dessou explained that if Leo and Victor had not taken the bulk of their art out of the country it would have been there when Goebbels ordered all of the art to be sold, the money to be applied toward the *Führermuseum*, Hitler's mammoth museum of art to be constructed in Austria. Hermann Göring enlisted several French dealers to sell the paintings.

"Alain Blanche was approached, but refused, which put his own life in jeopardy," Hammerstein said.

After the war, Dessou explained, Victor remained in America and opened his own gallery that still exists in the family, but operated independently. Leo returned to Paris and, together with their partner Alain Blanche, went back to work.

"My grandfather died in 1960," Hammerstein said. "At which point my father took over the gallery. He died in 1990. That's when I took over. I am telling you all this in an effort to make clear that, if there was anything questionable about this gallery, I would know." He gestured to *Madame* Dessou. "We would know. We take stolen Nazi art quite seriously here."

The history lesson offered little comfort. All of it could have been either fabricated or whitewashed. A fancy leather album proved nothing.

I thanked them both for their time and stood.

"What are you planning on doing?" Hammerstein asked.

"I have no choice. Interpol will have to be involved."

I wanted to see what that threat meant to Hammerstein.

But he only shrugged and said, "That seems prudent, under the circumstances. However—"

I waited for what would come next.

"Might I have the rest of the day to make some discreet inquires? I may be able to learn some things you, or the authorities, could not. If by the end of the day I am unsuccessful, then by all means call them."

That sounded reasonable. Especially since I was at a dead end. I thanked him, we traded cell phone numbers, and I called my driver, who picked me up on the street.

"Drop me at the d'Orsay museum."

I needed to think, so a nice quiet museum seemed a good place to do it.

"A round-about way too," I said. "Let's make sure we don't have any followers."

I spent the better part of an hour at a new exhibit of Bonnard paintings that Marlene and Spencer Hays, an American couple, had donated to the d'Orsay two years before. The art did a lot to lift my spirits. Not many paintings make me laugh, but these were so delightful that for a little while I was transported to an earlier era in Paris, before world wars and terrorist attacks. When the City of Lights shined. On my way out, I stopped in the museum bookstore. I'd never read much about Bonnard, and the show had made me curious. I was rifling through the books assembled on the artist when I spotted something on a different subject.

A Pack of Thieves: How Hitler Plundered Europe and the Jews With the Greatest Theft in History.

I bought it along with the Bonnard catalogue raisonné and returned to my room at the hotel. I ordered a pot of hot chocolate and a croissant and settled in to read, hoping that even though only half a day had passed, Hammerstein would find out something soon and call.

Inside the Bonnard book I scanned the index and found something. One of the paintings described in the text belonged to the collection of Robert Travers.

Interesting.

Then, in the book about Hitler plundering the art world, I saw that a Swiss banking firm of Travers & Caleche was named as helping the Nazis to store plundered art stolen from Jews.

I switched to my phone and used the search engine to learn that Travers & Caleche existed until around 1948, when the firm went out of business. The Travers mentioned was Nathan Travers, but nothing connected him with Robert Travers.

Coincidence?

I doubted it.

I kept reading.

Around 4:00 p.m. Cotton called.

I took him through what I knew so far and about what happened to both me and Miguel.

"Travers is a client of Hammerstein's," I said. "I'm sure of that. My father was a client of Hammerstein's and of Travers', through the Repository. The dots are connecting, but they don't form a picture yet."

"I'm more concerned about somebody trying to kill you."

"They are going to have to try a lot harder."

"That's my girl."

"And what *are* you doing in Poland?"

"Stuff I should probably not be doing. You want me to come there?"

"I don't need a man to save me."

"That's not what I meant, and you know it. How about just a little help?"

"I got this. Do whatever it is you are doing, then tell me about it this weekend."

I was scheduled to fly to Copenhagen for a few days. We alternated making the trip. He came to France one time, I went to Denmark the next.

"I'm looking forward to it," he said.

"So am I."

We ended the call with *I love yous*, which was nice to hear.

I went back to the Hitler book and flipped through to the photo pages at its center.

My phone rang.

An unknown number.

I answered anyway.

"*Mademoiselle* Vitt," a female voice said. "I work with *Monsieur* Hammerstein. He wanted me to tell you that his inquiries have borne fruit. There is someone you should talk with. She might prove most helpful."

Chapter 18

THE MARAIS IS AN ECLECTIC NEIGHBORHOOD IN THE 4TH Arrondissement. I'd visited the Place des Vosges, the 17th century elegant quadrangle of mansard roofed buildings with a central green, often. But the address I'd been provided was on Rue des Rosiers, in a section I wasn't familiar with. Fine houses dating from centuries ago lined the principal streets. I lightly rapped on the wooden door for one identified as 468. When answered, *Madame* Dessou from the gallery stood in the doorway.

My senses went to ultra-high alert.

"I know this is a surprise. My full name is Eloise Lavertu Dessou. I'm a copyist. I knew your father."

"So why not just tell me that at the gallery?"

"That would have been impossible."

I caught the hesitation. "Because of Hammerstein?"

She nodded. "Would you like to come in?"

Hardly. "I don't think so."

She seemed to understand my apprehension. "All right. Let's walk down the street. There's a bistro there where we can speak. In public."

We entered the café and took a table toward the rear. Only a handful of others were there. I'd brought my gun, which rested reassuringly at the base of my spine beneath my jacket.

"Please, order something," she said. "The Dover sole and aligot is delicious and I have a long story to tell you."

The waiter brought a basket filled with chunks of baguette and took our orders. Two soles and a potato and cheese dish. *Madame* Dessou ordered a bottle of the house white wine.

"My assistant placed the call to you," she said.

"Has Hammerstein done anything since I left?"

She shrugged. "I have no idea. He and I are not that close."

"Care to explain?"

"I will. Please, be patient."

I decided to try something else. "Are you an art forger?"

She grinned. "No. I am a copyist. There is a difference. The manner in which I create copies prevents them from being resold as originals."

I was curious. "How so?"

"I sign them on the back."

"You copied my father's paintings?"

She nodded.

"There was no signature on the back of the one copy I examined."

"Your father did not want me to sign them. He preferred the complete illusion that the paintings were all authentic. I made a rare exception."

The waiter brought the wine and poured. *Madame* Dessou lifted her glass to me. "*Santé.*"

"*Santé*," I echoed, then sipped the crisp, mellow wine.

"Typically, my clients want to keep the originals safe, but they also want the pleasure of living with beautiful art."

"Is that how you met my father?"

She nodded. "Like many of *Monsieur* Hammerstein's clients, he told me that he wanted a visual memory of what he'd paid so dearly for and loved so much. Over a period of nine years I copied each of the fifteen paintings he purchased."

A surprising revelation.

"Does Hammerstein know?"

She shook her head. "That was between me and your father."

I had a million questions, but I decided to let this woman tell me in her own way and in her own time.

The waiter brought our food.

The fish was fresh and delicate, perfectly seasoned. The whipped potatoes with melted cheese delicious. No heavy spices or garlic. Just the way I liked it.

"I haven't eaten much in the last twenty-four hours," I said. "And this is excellent." I enjoyed another bite of fish. "How long have you worked for the gallery?"

"Thirty-three years. But I'm not staff. My husband and I worked only when needed."

"Is he a copyist?"

"He was a restorer. I both copy and restore."

I caught the past tense and asked the obvious.

"He died some time ago."

I told her I was sorry, then recalled the show back at the gallery. "What about being the resident historian?"

"That was a recent assignment. I came up with the idea a few years ago and offered to create that album. It allowed me the opportunity to learn a great deal about the gallery. As you saw, *Monsieur* Hammerstein is quite proud of his family's legacy."

"How did you become a copyist?"

She smiled. "It's difficult to make a steady income as an artist. A fickle world, at best. Success can be fleeting. I have watched too many of my friends struggle. My husband and I wanted a more…bourgeois existence."

I caught the hesitation. "Is that the only reason?"

"You are most astute," she said. "Like your father, in so many ways. I can explain that part of the story better…after dinner. I would like to take you to an exhibit that is opening soon. It is nearby. It will be easier to explain everything there."

This whole thing stunk. Bad. I was being manipulated. And not with much subtlety. But like Cotton would say, *to catch the fox you have to follow the dogs.*

"All right," I said.

After the main course we had tarte tatin with crème anglaise, a perfect light and sweet ending to a good meal. We followed that with some strong espresso.

"I have to ask," she said as we drank the coffee. "Do you really not know anything about your father's paintings?"

"I had no idea about any of this until two days ago."

"So you do not know why they were copied?"

I shook my head.

"That's interesting. Because your father specifically told me that he was going to explain it all to you. It was important to him that you knew about the copies. He hoped you would understand."

I was puzzled. "Understand what?"

"Why he wasn't leaving you the fortune that each of those fifteen masterpieces was worth."

Chapter 19

I TRIED TO COMPREHEND WHAT SHE'D SAID. "ARE YOU SAYING *HE* TOOK those paintings from the repository?"

She nodded. "That's correct. There was no theft."

I desperately wanted to know. "Do you know what my father did with them?"

Madame Dessou glared at me with the studied eye of an artist. Sizing me up. "Of course. Why else would we be speaking?"

Good point.

"Come. I will show you."

We paid the bill and left.

Outside, we turned right on Rue des Rosiers. Halfway down the block we reached a metal gate at number 10. Past the wrought iron I glimpsed a long stone alley. A plaque on the stone pillar identified the site as the Jardin des Rosiers-Joseph Migneret.

"Have you ever seen the little garden here?" she asked.

I shook my head.

"It's closed now. But it's lovely. If you walk by here during the day, you should stop in. It's named for Joseph Migneret, an elementary school principal and resistance fighter, who, during the war, sheltered hundreds of Jewish students threatened with deportation."

I read the writing on the plaque.

Over 11,400 Jewish children were deported from France between 1942 and 1944, all murdered at Auschwitz. Of them, more than 500 had lived right here in this neighborhood. A hundred of them were too young to ever have attended school. I felt a lump in my throat, the last line asked anyone reading the plaque to remember the names of the *little ones* because *your memory is their sole resting place.*

"My grandmother was one of the children who survived those horrors," she said in a whisper. "Her baby brother was not as lucky."

"I'm sorry," I said, knowing how hollow my words were in the face of what her family had endured.

"The enormity of the evil that man is capable of inflicting on his fellow man never fails to render me speechless," she said. "Animals, who only kill each other to eat or protect their young, are more humane than our species has ever proven to be. We kill for no reason at all."

I stayed silent.

"Come," she said, pointing down the street.

We walked for another few minutes down Rue du Roi de Sicile, then turned a few corners until we found Rue Geoffroy l'Asnier. *Madame* Dessou stopped in front of a white stone building set back from the street. It definitely appeared more recent than the structures around it. An electronic iron gate blocked any entrance, the portcullis formidable, the bars as thick as a man's index finger. A small sign above a call box requested that any visitor push the button and ask permission to enter.

"Have you ever been here?" she asked.

"Never," I told her. "Where are we?"

"The Mémorial de la Shoah. Paris's Holocaust museum."

The name rang a bell. The invitation I'd received a few days ago. Wanting me to attend an opening. That was way too much a coincidence.

"You sent me the invitation?" I asked.

"I did."

"Why?"

"It was important you come. But since you are here two days early, I felt it best to speak with you now."

"Are we going inside?"

She nodded.

That could be a problem. Surely there was high security. Metal detectors. Bag screening. Guards. No way I was going to escape that scrutiny with a gun nestled to my spine.

A buzzer sounded and I heard the iron gate release.

Neither one of us had used the call box. Somebody was watching and knew my guide. We stepped into a forecourt that supported a large circular memorial. I noticed the writing on its side. The names of the various German death camps and the Warsaw Ghetto. On the building, above the forecourt, were two carved inscriptions.

Remember what Amalek did unto our generation,
which exterminated 600 myriad bodies and souls
even though there was no war.

Madame Dessou noticed my interest.

"An adaptation of Deuteronomy 25:17," she said.

The second inscription was longer.

Before the unknown Jewish martyr,
incline your head in piety and respect for all the martyrs.
Incline your thoughts to accompany them along their path of sorrow.
They will lead you to the highest pinnacle of justice and truth.

"A quote from Justin Godart, Minister of Health and Honorary President of the Committee for the Unknown Jewish Martyr," she said.

A passageway ahead led toward the main building.

Countless names filled the walls.

"Listed there are 76,000 French Jews who were deported and murdered by the Nazis. Alphabetically, by year of their deportation," she said.

Incredible.

And powerful.

The screech of tires from beyond the gate interrupted my thoughts. I whirled around to see a vehicle grind to a stop just outside the iron bars.

Its rear window down.

A gun barrel aimed my way.

Chapter 20

I DOVE TOWARD *MADAME* DESSOU AND TOOK US BOTH DOWN TO THE pavement. A volley of automatic weapon fire raked the courtyard, but its span was limited by the width of the locked gate. A few of the rounds pinged off the iron bars, ricocheting in all directions. I kept the older woman down and reached back for my own gun. I rolled to my right and pointed it at the car. Three pulls of the trigger sent bullets toward the open window. One of the rounds found the metal bars.

But there was no return fire.

The car sped away.

I sprang to my feet just as two security guards rushed from the museum, guns drawn.

"Are you okay?" I asked Dessou.

She nodded fast, clearly shaken.

"Stay here."

I rushed toward the gate and saw the car, a dark Citroën, speeding toward the end of the street.

"I need this open," I called out, hoping somebody was listening.

The buzzer rang.

I pulled the gate inward and stepped out to the sidewalk. Two taxis were parked against the curb a few meters away. One was empty. The other occupied. I ran up and yanked open the driver's side door. The older man saw the gun and the look on my face. Shock filled his eyes and he rolled from the car, muttering in French *not to hurt him*. I jumped inside, slammed the door shut, and floored the accelerator. My target was about to disappear around the corner ahead. I sped toward it, firing once out the open window at the receding taillights. I came to the same intersection and yanked the steering wheel hard left, the wheels skidding across the pavement as I took the turn.

Too fast.

The back end kept swaying.

I used a mixture of brake and accelerator to stop the spin in time and regain control. I'd been taught the move at that security school by an instructor with penchant for high-speed driving.

The hood was now pointed where I wanted to go.

I revved the engine and accelerated.

The Citroën and I were now on a busier boulevard. Four-laned, with a treed concrete medium between. Traffic began to congeal. The Citroën shot out of its lane and crossed the medium into opposing traffic.

A daring maneuver.

I had no choice but to follow.

Horns blared.

Oncoming vehicles swerved out of the Citroën's way. The only good thing was it was clearing a path for me. Which I took, gaining on my target. I kept wedging in and out, overtaking the cars, then squeezing back into the counter flow. The Citroën was now close, so I stuck my left arm out the window and fired a round, which obliterated the rear windshield, spraying pebbles of safety glass through the interior.

That should get their attention.

The Citroën decided to quit going against the flow and re-crossed the medium.

I followed.

Traffic was thinner now, which allowed for more speed. I tried to get my bearings and realized we were nearing the Seine, headed into the heart of the city where cars would be far more plentiful.

Slowing things down.

I just needed to keep pace.

The Citroën was now about fifty meters ahead, still accelerating, weaving in and out between the cars.

Suddenly, its brake lights lit and the car slowed.

My speed allowed for a fast approach.

Thirty meters.

Twenty.

I saw someone whirl around in the open space where the rear window had been and aim the automatic rifle my way.

Ten meters.

I veered the car hard left and hit the accelerator, moving into the inner lane.

The rifle fired.

A spray of rounds caught the passenger's side of the windshield, shattering the glass with spiderwebs. I was now past the Citroën, which had changed lanes too, headed my way. Someone emerged from one of the windows and started firing. Damn. Where were the police? Surely someone had called them by now considering the havoc that had been wreaked on this road.

I slowed and allowed the traffic in the outer lane to catch up, including the Citroën, which raced past. I caught a quick look. A driver with two passengers. One in the front seat, the other in the back toting the weapon. I returned to the outer lane with a car between me and the Citroën.

An intersection loomed ahead, as did an arched bridge, one of many that crossed the Seine. The traffic signal was red to me, cars whizzing by perpendicular, blocking the way ahead. The Citroën seemed unfazed and barreled into the flow, slowing and weaving a path through, horns blaring in protest.

Which opened an alley for me.

Enough with the games.

I sped up and plowed the front end of my car into the Citroën's rear bumper, sending the vehicle lurching forward. I apparently caught the driver off guard as he'd not tried to flee, surely recovering from the unexpected blow.

Then the Citroën started to move away.

But not fast enough.

The arched stone bridge lay ahead, traffic heavy in the opposite lane, but our two lanes were thin enough with cars to allow me to come parallel to the Citroën. We both sped onto the bridge, its side walls low to the river below, a sidewalk separating the curb from the bridge's edge. I was hoping the Citroën would make the mistake and speed up.

Which it did.

I matched it, but stayed right beside the other vehicle.

I whipped the wheel to the right, banging into the Citroën. Cotton liked to tell me what his mother sometimes said. *You're only helpless when your nail polish is wet, but even then you can still pull the trigger if you have to.*

Damn right.

I slammed into the Citroën two more times. We were still on the upside of the arch. *Timing wasn't everything. It was absolutely everything.* So I added speed and kept ramming, driving the Citroën further right, onto the sidewalk, toward the low wall that bordered the edge.

We came toward the arch's apex.

Time to pull the trigger.

I added one last slam.

Hard.

With added momentum from the accelerator.

The Citroën swerved out of control, its forward acceleration and bridge's upslope enough to send it airborne. The wheels climbed the short stone wall, propelling the vehicle out into the open air, plunging it downward to the river.

I hit the brakes and screeched to a halt.

Other cars had already stopped.

People were out, leaning over the stone balustrade, staring down into the murky river where the car bobbed like a cork.

Then it sank.

Three heads popped from the surface.

And sirens were approaching.

Chapter 21

TWELVE DAYS HAD PASSED SINCE I'D READ THE STORY ABOUT THE robbery at my friends' Provence house and received the invitation in the mail for an exhibit in Paris. I hadn't thought I'd be in the City of Lights for the event but, as it turned out, I was.

At *Madame* Dessou's request I arrived at the Mémorial de la Shoah an hour earlier than the official opening. She'd said she wanted to take me through the exhibit without any crowds. For the second time, she was going to try to show me something that she'd assured me my father would want me to see.

This evening I brought no gun. Instead, I was dressed in a black Chanel long-sleeved dress, matching jacket, and black suede Louboutin boots. *Madame* Dessou waited for me at the security checkpoint. She too was dressed in a stunning black sheath that set off her ivory skin. We'd seen each other at the hospital the night of the incident, and then the next day at the police department.

It seemed that Lucien Hammerstein and Robert Travers were not mere acquittances. They were coconspirators in crime.

The three men fished from the Seine all talked, linking them to Hammerstein, who'd hired their services to kill me. Once confronted, Hammerstein admitted that his gallery had hidden dozens of paintings and prints in the Repository—all plundered by Nazis during World War II.

Contrary to what I'd been told, the authorities had learned that Travers maintained duplicate keys to every one of his clients' vaults. Which allowed him easy access to remove whatever he wanted. Replacing the wax seals on the doors turned out to be simple, since the Repository maintained the brass stamps. One current, and two former employees, all on Travers' payroll, cracked, and it was learned that Travers often visited his clients' vaults to have copies made of some of their paintings, drawings, prints, sculptures and jewels, taking the originals for himself.

The entire scam had made the front pages of newspapers around the world, drawing a lot of attention to Andorra's tax haven status. Hammerstein was arrested. In addition, the scandal exposed several museums across Europe and Asia that had purchased paintings from Hammerstein, who'd acted as Travers' broker on the world stage. All of those institutions would soon be involved in reparation lawsuits.

Travers remained at large, staying on his yacht, avoiding territorial waters and only going ashore in places where there was no fear of arrest or extradition. His last reported whereabouts was Libya. The Repository had been raided and the vaults all unsealed. What was there to be found?

The authorities had yet to release any details.

Still, with all those revelations, I remained totally in the dark about my father's collection. Esmerelda knew precious little. Thankfully, she and I had made our peace, my godmother beginning to understand that I could indeed handle myself under pressure.

Where were the original paintings? Had Travers stolen and resold them? Was he keeping them for himself? And then there was that cryptic comment *Madame* Dessou had said the day of the attack, suggesting my father had other plans for the paintings and he'd personally removed the originals. I wanted to believe that the paintings would resurface and that I'd be able to do what I'd wanted to do all along—donate them to two worthy museums.

But I was still short on facts.

"How is your arm?" I asked *Madame* Dessou as we greeted each other.

She'd injured it when I took her to the ground.

"It's much better. The doctor said I'll only have a faint scar. But so many of us have such worse scars. My grandmother had a tattoo on her arm her whole life."

I realized what she meant.

The mark of the Nazis forced on to innocents.

We passed the museum's security checkpoint and entered the memorial.

I followed her through a set of double locking doors into an inner courtyard, immediately feeling a sense of being interred.

I told her of the sensation.

"That is exactly what the architect wanted you to feel." She gestured with a sad smile. "This is our Holocaust museum. President Chirac had it built in this section of Paris because this is where the majority of the Jewish population lived at the beginning of World War II. Many of us still live here on the same streets, in the same houses where the Nazis rounded up our families."

She looked away.

To give her a moment of privacy I examined a large sculpture in front of us. The bronze cylinder had oxidized green with exposure to the elements. On it were raised letters spelling out the names of places that I recognized. Camps where Jews had been incarcerated and murdered by the millions.

Auschwitz. Belzec. Bergen-Belsen. Birkenau. Buchenwald. Chelmno. Dachau. Majdanek. Mauthausen. Sobibor. Struthof. Treblinka.

I shivered in the cool night air, not wanting to be here but realizing that I had to. I was an avid student of the past. My life was devoted to recreating it in my castle rebuilding project. I'd visited the Holocaust memorial in Washington D.C. My father and I once toured Auschwitz on a wet, bitterly cold winter day. We'd walked the paths and seen the crematorium. He'd told me that day that if we are going to survive as a civilization, we can never forget and never allow any of it to happen again. But there was something more profound and personal here, with this woman, in this neighborhood, where her grandmother and all of her family had been taken away to die.

And what did any of this have to do with my father?

If he'd bought paintings with suspect provenances, if some of his collection had been plundered and looted from Jews by Nazis, I had to believe he was ignorant of the fact. Never would he have profited from such suffering.

Never.

Madame Dessou escorted me inside.

We stood before a recreation from the front of the concentration camp barracks in the Warsaw Ghetto.

She examined her watch. "We have an hour. Enough time for me to show you what you need to see."

We walked down a hallway, its walls rough rock, then descended a flight of stairs to a crypt. There, a large underground room was suffused with a warm, yellow glow from hidden lighting illuminating more stone walls. A large black marble Star of David sculpture filled a floor depression in the center, an everlasting flame burning at its base.

"This is a symbolic burial site for the six million Jews killed in the war and who do not have a grave," she told me. "Buried under this star are ashes of Jews taken from all of the death camps and mingled together."

We stood for a moment of silence, then I followed *Madame* Dessou out of the room and into an enclave with floor to ceiling wooden shelves. Behind the glass that kept them safe, were hundreds of perfectly lined-up colored boxes holding thousands of stacked manila colored cards.

"This is the Jewish file," she said.

I stared at the cards.

"These are the records compiled by the Prefecture of Police from 1941 to 1944. They list the name of every man, woman, and child who was arrested in Paris, as well as those held at all the camps in the Loiret region. Here, safely stored, so they will never be forgotten."

"This is overwhelming," I said.

"I know," she said, nodding then taking my hand. "But it's important that you see it. Let's go back upstairs. I have something else to show you."

We reclimbed the stairs.

"The exhibit opening tonight is here, in this gallery."

We walked through an open portal, above which hung a sign.

Le Marché de l'Art sous l'Occupation.

The Art Market During the Occupation.

From the invitation.

"This show examines the history of the French art market during the years of the occupation from 1940 to 1944. At the reception later on you'll see the curator of the show, my friend Emanuelle Polack, present the director of the Louvre with a restitution claim. The museum had loaned us several paintings for this show. But the heirs of the Jewish owners of three of those works are suing the Louvre to return the paintings to them."

"That's going to happen here?" I asked.

"In about an hour." She smiled. "I'm on the board of the memorial, so I have the inside scoop."

"What a moment that's going to be."

"Sadly, it's the only way to garner any attention these days to the issue. And that will be just the beginning. This show is guaranteed to stir up trouble. Do you know much about the art market during the war?"

"I've been trying to catch up, but mostly I've only learned how much I don't know."

She smiled at my honesty. "While the war raged, while millions were interred and murdered, there was a thriving art market at work. Starting in 1941 the French government—under Nazi control and Vichy laws—stole everything they could from Jews. They took their businesses, bank accounts, homes, jewels, and art. While the Jews languished in internment camps starving and dying, auction houses and galleries made money off that plunder. The estimates are that over 700,000 paintings alone were taken from Jews during the war. Over 100,000 of those are still missing."

I began to dread what *Madame* Dessou was telling me.

"Come look at this," she said, once again taking me by the hand.

She drew me over to a corner of the exhibit and a wall filled with photographs of an auction being conducted.

One I recognized.

From the invitation I'd received.

"Why didn't you just contact me directly?" I asked. "Why the subterfuge?"

"It had to be that way. I could not risk Hammerstein learning anything about me."

Which made sense.

"This new exhibit seemed the perfect time to connect with you. Of course, I had no knowledge that you would discover the fakes on your own, along with all that ultimately was revealed," she said. "I assure you, if I had, things would have been handled differently."

I appreciated her concern.

"Look at this," she said, motioning to one of the black and white images of the Charpentier auctioneer holding up a painting for the dapper, well-dressed audience to bid on. But in this one I could see the actual painting.

The Monet my father owned.

I stepped closer.

"You're seeing it right," she said. "And that's not the only one you might recognize."

She pointed to another photo in which several men were examining a Chagall.

My father's.

A sick feeling invaded my stomach.

My father had owned paintings that had been stolen from Jews who'd perished in camps, or escaped, only to never recover their belongings.

She led me to a glass showcase.

Inside were bills of sale on yellowed paper, written in fading ink.

I recognized more names of artists. "Are these the documents missing from my father's collection?"

She nodded.

I could not believe what I was seeing. What I was coming to understand. My father had been the most principled man I'd ever known. So much so that those ideals eventually came between us. Especially when it came to religion. Had he really bought stolen paintings from Hammerstein, knowing where they'd come from? I made no effort to hide the shock and disgust I was feeling.

"This is not what you think," she said. "Please. Come with me. There are some people you must meet."

She ushered me out, past more cabinets and display cases, down a long corridor and into a room set up with wine and other refreshments. People were already assembled. I was in no mood to meet anyone. I'd just learned, after two weeks of wondering, that my father had bought art that had the blood of innocents upon it.

A woman approached, maybe in her late thirties, and *Madame* Dessou made an introduction. "Cassiopeia, this is Mary Weiss." We were joined by another woman, this one a bit older, in her fifties. "This is Jillian Greenfield."

I shook her hand.

For the next few moments, much to my discomfort, I met a dozen men and women of all ages. *Madame* Dessou then lifted two flutes of champagne, handing one to me.

"Everyone," she said. "I would like to drink to the memory of Arturo Pedro Cristóbal Vitt. A humanitarian and a hero." She turned to me, her glass still held aloft. "Your father did buy every one of those paintings knowing they were stolen. Knowing they belonged to someone who had lost his or her life in the camps, or someone who had traded their art trying to save a family, a child, a wife, a mother, a father. What you don't know is that he bought every one of them in order to return them to their rightful owners. Altogether he spent millions of dollars. He then returned each and every one of them. These people here tonight are members of the families he returned them to."

I was stunned.

I stood there looking at the faces.

Thinking how one of history's greatest atrocities had touched them all.

"Your father," *Madame* Dessou said, "contacted our network. We have many people who work for different museums and galleries. He let us know that he would buy any painting Hammerstein was offering with a troubled provenance. There were fifteen. Once your father purchased a work, he had me paint a copy. That way the painting could be displayed in his home and no one would be the wiser as to the original. Especially Hammerstein. He then placed the original in the Repository while we searched for the heirs. This was before Travers began looting the vaults. That started shortly after your father died. So that's why there was nothing but empty frames in Andorra. Your father had given all the paintings away by the time of his death."

I was stunned.

"He wanted you to know," the older woman said. "I'm only sorry he never got to tell you himself. He told me something once. Something I never forgot. From his Book of Mormon. *Now ye may suppose that this is foolishness in me, but behold I say unto you, that by small and simple things are great things brought to pass.* He was so right. I sent the invitation as a means to get you to come to this exhibition so we could tell you."

A memory flooded my brain.

A long ago afternoon.

My father and I sitting in the gallery at the villa, looking at the paintings.

Of all the things I have ever done, the two I am most proud of are being your father and owning these paintings.

I had been a bit offended, being placed in the same category as canvas and paint, no matter who the artist might have been. So I told him how I felt. But he merely leaned over and kissed me on the brow.

One day, you won't be insulted at all.

That day had come.

I raised my glass.

"To *papá*. And all that he did."

Writer's Note

Steve has always wanted to include Andorra in a novel. It's a fascinating place, straight from the Middle Ages, a land that retains much of its storied antiquity. If you ever have the chance, pay Andorra a visit. All of the other locales in the story are likewise real. Only the House of Long Ago, where Cassiopeia was raised, is our creation.

Stolen art is big business. At the end of World War II, the Allies found plundered artwork in more than one thousand repositories across Germany and Austria. Nearly 700,000 pieces were identified and returned to the countries from which they were taken. Those governments were then supposed to locate the original owners and return the art. Unfortunately, thousands of pieces either never made it back to the rightful owners or the owners could not be tracked down.

Finally, in 1985, inventory lists of works of art that had been confiscated from Jews began to be released to the public. That effort went worldwide in 1998 when thirty-nine nations signed a joint pledge to identify art stolen from Holocaust victims and to compensate their heirs. But despite all this, hundreds of thousands of pieces are still unaccounted for, some of them famed masterpieces. We thought you might like to see the top 10 most valuable works of art still missing:

(1) Raphael, *Portrait of a Young Man* (1513). Poland's most famous art loss from the war. The painting was taken in 1939 from the Czartoryskis' family collection in Kraków, intent on becoming part of Hitler's *Führermuseum.* It disappeared at the end of the war.

(2) The Amber Room (18th Century). A thirty-foot square room sheathed in six tons of jewel-grade amber. It was looted in 1941 and taken to the city of Königsberg, never seen after 1945. The Soviets completed a replica of the room in 2003. It now stands in the Catherine's Palace outside St. Petersburg, Russia. Steve dealt with this lost treasure in his novel, *The Amber Room* (2003).

(3) Vincent van Gogh, *The Painter on the Road to Tarascon* (1888). Among van Gogh's most cherished pieces, it was thought to have burned when the Allies bombed the town of Magdeburg, destroying the museum that housed it. But no one knows if the painting was inside at the time.

(4) Giovanni Bellini, *Madonna with Child* (1430). The painting was evacuated in the early 1940s from a museum in Berlin, housed in a flak tower that eventually came within Soviet control. Most of the objects in that tower were either looted or presumed destroyed, but no one knows for sure.

(5) Gustav Klimt, *Portrait of Trude Steiner* (1900). Seized by the Nazis in 1938 and subsequently sold to an unknown individual in 1941, it has never been seen since. Klimt is a personal favorite of M.J.'s.

(6) Rembrandt van Rijn, *An Angel with Titus' Features* (17th century). Stolen from a French chateau in 1943, it was taken to Paris and also set aside for Hitler's *Führermuseum,* along with 332 other works. Eventually, 162 of those were found but not this painting, which is still missing.

(7) Peter Paul Rubens, *The Annunciation* (1609). This disappeared after it was forcibly sold through a Berlin art auctioneer in 1935.

(8) Canaletto, *Piazza Santa Margherita* (18th century). Seized from the private collection of a gallery owner who fled to the Netherlands in 1940, parts of that collection were eventually returned but the hunt is still on for this painting.

(9) Edgar Degas, *Five Dancing Women* (19th century). The Nazis acquired this pastel drawing when they stole the collection of a Jewish art patron. After the war his heirs filed a lawsuit against Hungary seeking the return of the collection, but this work is still gone.

(10) Pissarro, *The Boulevard Montmartre, Twilight* (1897). Part of a collection looted by the Nazis and subsequently sold through a Swiss art dealer in 1941. Its current location remains unknown.

An impressive list of masterpieces.

And lest you think that all this missing art is most likely gone forever, in November 2013 German authorities announced the discovery of about 1,500 works confiscated by the Nazis. They were found in a Munich apartment belonging to the son of Hildebrand Gurlitt, one of Hermann Goering's art dealers commissioned to liquidate so-called degenerate art. The works, by artists including Picasso, Matisse, and Chagall, were estimated to be worth about $1.35 billion. Determining their rightful owners has been an ongoing process and will take years to complete.

But the question remains.

How much more is still out there, waiting to be found?

This story deals with art owners intentionally producing copies of their purchased works. This is not unusual. And the displaying of copies while the originals are safely locked away happens for a variety of reasons. Sometimes the act is mere vanity, allowing the owner to show off a "Claude Monet or Picasso," when in reality it is nothing more than a copy. Is this practice forgery? Not really. Copyists are careful not to produce something that could be mistaken by an expert for the original and, as noted in Chapter 18, most sign their name to the back of their work, something no forger would ever do.

The Holocaust museum in Paris exists (chapters 19 and 21). About 300,000 Jews were living in France in the late 1930s. Within months after France's June 1940 armistice with Germany, new laws led to Jews being excluded from professional life and dispossessed of their property. In collaboration with the Germans, the Vichy government, along with local and state French police, began rounding up Jews in 1941. In 1995, French president Jacques Chirac officially recognized France's responsibility for this atrocity. Ten years later, Chirac inaugurated the Shoah Memorial and Holocaust Center.

As described in the story (chapter 19), the names of the death camps are engraved on a circular memorial in the courtyard, along with the words of Justin Godard, a former government minister and honorary president of the Committee for the Unknown Jewish Martyr. The center combines a museum, a documentation center and reading room, France's largest (by number of titles) physical bookstore on the subject of the Holocaust, an auditorium, symposia, and a memorial crypt. An estimated 78,000 Jewish men, women and children were deported from France between 1942 and 1944 to Auschwitz. Of them 76,000 did not return. As Cassiopeia discovered, past the security box at the entrance from the street, there's a narrow passage where the walls are inscribed with the names and dates of birth of every one of these 76,000 individuals.

A powerful and moving memorial designed with one thing in mind.

To never forget.

Also from M.J. Rose and Steve Berry

The Museum of Mysteries
A Cassiopeia Vitt Adventure
By Steve Berry and M.J. Rose
Now available!

Cassiopeia Vitt takes center stage in this exciting novella from New York Times bestsellers M.J. Rose and Steve Berry.

In the French mountain village of Eze, Cassiopeia visits an old friend who owns and operates the fabled Museum of Mysteries, a secretive place of the odd and arcane. When a robbery occurs at the museum, Cassiopeia gives chase to the thief and is plunged into a firestorm.

Through a mix of modern day intrigue and ancient alchemy, Cassiopeia is propelled back and forth through time, the inexplicable journeys leading her into a hotly contested French presidential election. Both candidates harbor secrets they would prefer to keep quiet, but an ancient potion could make that impossible. With intrigue that begins in southern France and ends in a chase across the streets of Paris, this magical, fast-paced, hold-your-breath thriller is all you've come to expect from M.J. Rose and Steve Berry.

The Lake of Learning
A Cassiopeia Vitt Adventure
By Steve Berry and M.J. Rose
Now available!

For over a decade Cassiopeia Vitt has been building an authentic French castle, using only materials and techniques from the 13th century. But when a treasure is unearthed at the construction site—an ancient Book of Hours—a multitude of questions are raised, all pointing to an ancient and forgotten religious sect.

Once the Cathars existed all across southern France, challenging

Rome and attracting the faithful by the tens of thousands. Eventually, in 1208, the Pope declared them heretics and ordered a crusade—the first where Christians killed Christians—and thousands were slaughtered, the Cathars all but exterminated. Now a piece of that past has re-emerged, one that holds the key to the hiding place of the most precious object the Cathars possessed. And when more than one person becomes interested in that secret, in particular a thief and a billionaire, the race is on.

From the medieval walled city of Carcassonne, to the crest of mysterious Montségur, to a forgotten cavern beneath the Pyrenees, Cassiopeia is drawn deeper and deeper into a civil war between two people obsessed with revenge and murder.

The Last Tiara

By M.J. Rose
Coming February 2, 2021

From *New York Times* and *Wall Street Journal* bestseller M.J. Rose comes a provocative and moving story of a young female architect in post-World War II Manhattan, who stumbles upon a hidden treasure and begins a journey to discovering her mother's life during the fall of the Romanovs.

Sophia Moon had always been reticent about her life in Russia and when she dies, suspiciously, on a wintry New York evening, Isobelle despairs that her mother's secrets have died with her. But while renovating the apartment they shared, Isobelle discovers something among her mother's effects—a stunning silver tiara, stripped of its jewels.

Isobelle's research into the tiara's provenance draws her closer to her mother's past—including the story of what became of her father back in Russia, a man she has never known. The facts elude her until she meets a young jeweler, who wants to help her but is conflicted by his loyalty to the Midas Society, a covert international organization whose mission is to return lost and stolen antiques, jewels, and artwork to their original owners.

Told in alternating points of view, the stories of the two young women unfurl as each struggles to find their way during two separate wars. In 1915, young Sofiya Petrovitch, favorite of the royal household and best friend of Grand Duchess Olga Nikolaevna, tends to wounded soldiers in a makeshift hospital within the grounds of the Winter Palace in St. Petersburg and finds the love of her life. In 1948 New York, Isobelle Moon works to break through the rampant sexism of the age as one of very few women working in a male-dominated profession and discovers far more about love and family than she ever hoped for.

In M.J. Rose's deftly constructed narrative, the secrets of Sofiya's early life are revealed incrementally, even as Isobelle herself works to solve the mystery of the historic Romanov tiara (which is based on an actual Romanov artifact that is, to this day, still missing)—and how it is that her mother came to possess it. The two strands play off each other in finely-tuned counterpoint, building to a series of surprising and deeply satisfying revelations.

The Warsaw Protocol

A Cotton Malone Novel
By Steve Berry
Now Available

In *New York Times* bestseller Steve Berry's latest Cotton Malone adventure, one by one the seven precious relics of the Arma Christi, the weapons of Christ, are disappearing from sanctuaries across the world.

After former Justice Department agent Cotton Malone witnesses the theft of one of them, he learns from his old boss, Stephanie Nelle, that a private auction is about to be held where incriminating information on the president of Poland will be offered to the highest bidder—blackmail that both the United States and Russia want, but for vastly different reasons.

The price of admission to that auction is one of the relics, so Malone is first sent to a castle in Poland to steal the Holy Lance, a thousand-year-old spear sacred to not only Christians but to the Polish people, and then on to the auction itself. But nothing goes as planned and Malone is thrust into a bloody battle between three nations over information that, if exposed, could change the balance of power in Europe.

From the tranquil canals of Bruges, to the elegant rooms of Wawel Castle, to deep beneath the earth into an ancient Polish salt mine, Malone is caught in the middle of a deadly war—the outcome of which turns on a secret known as the Warsaw Protocol.

Cartier's Hope

By M.J. Rose
Now Available

From M.J. Rose, *New York Times* bestselling author of *Tiffany Blues*, "a lush, romantic historical mystery" (Kristin Hannah, *The Nightingale*), comes a gorgeously wrought novel of ambition and betrayal set in the Gilded Age.

New York, 1910: A city of extravagant balls in Fifth Avenue mansions and poor immigrants crammed into crumbling Lower East Side tenements. A city where the suffrage movement is growing stronger every day, but most women reporters are still delegated to the fashion and lifestyle pages. But Vera Garland is set on making her mark in a man's world of serious journalism.

Shortly after the world-famous Hope Diamond is acquired for a record sum, Vera begins investigating rumors about schemes by its new owner, jeweler Pierre Cartier, to manipulate its value. Vera is determined to find the truth behind the notorious diamond and its legendary curses—even better when the expose puts her in the same orbit as a magazine publisher whose blackmailing schemes led to the death of her beloved father.

Appealing to a young Russian jeweler for help, Vera is unprepared when she begins falling in love with him…and even more unprepared when she gets caught up in his deceptions and finds herself at risk of losing all she has worked so hard to achieve.

Set against the backdrop of New York's glitter and grit, of ruthless men and the atrocities they commit in the pursuit of power, this enthralling historical novel explores our very human needs for love, retribution—and to pursue one's destiny, regardless of the cost.

About Steve Berry

STEVE BERRY is the New York Times and #1 internationally bestselling author of fourteen Cotton Malone novels and four standalones. He has 25 million books in print, translated into 40 languages. With his wife, Elizabeth, he is the founder of History Matters, which is dedicated to historical preservation. He serves as an emeritus member on the Smithsonian Libraries Advisory Board and was a founding member of International Thriller Writers, formerly serving as its co-president.

About M.J. Rose

New York Times bestseller M.J. Rose grew up in New York City mostly in the labyrinthine galleries of the Metropolitan Museum, the dark tunnels and lush gardens of Central Park and reading her mother's favorite books before she was allowed. She believes mystery and magic are all around us but we are too often too busy to notice... books that exaggerate mystery and magic draw attention to it and remind us to look for it and revel in it.

Please visit her blog, Museum of Mysteries at http://www.mjrose.com/blog/

Rose's work has appeared in many magazines including *Oprah* magazine and she has been featured in the *New York Times, Newsweek, Wall Street Journal, Time, USA Today* and on the Today Show, and NPR radio. Rose graduated from Syracuse University, spent the '80s in advertising, has a commercial in the Museum of Modern Art in New York City and since 2005 has run the first marketing company for authors - Authorbuzz.com.

Rose lives in Connecticut with her husband, the musician and composer Doug Scofield.

Made in the USA
Monee, IL
01 July 2021